William—The Pirate

"LET'S KEEP HIM HERE," SAID WILLIAM. "AUNT JANE
WON'T KNOW."

(*See page 78*)

William—The Pirate

RICHMAL CROMPTON

Illustrated by Thomas Henry

MACMILLAN CHILDREN'S BOOKS

First published 1932

The illustrations by Thomas Henry
are reproduced
by permission of the
Hamlyn Group Picture Library

First published in this edition 1985 by

MACMILLAN CHILDREN'S BOOKS
A division of Macmillan Publishers Limited
London and Basingstoke
Associated companies throughout the world

Phototypeset by Wyvern Typesetting Limited, Bristol
Printed in Great Britain by Cox & Wyman Ltd

British Library Cataloguing in Publication Data

Crompton, Richmal
William—the pirate.
Rn: Richmal Crompton Lamburn   I. Title
823'.912[J]   PZ7
ISBNs: paperback 0–333–38904–2
hardback 0–333–38903–4

Contents

An invitation from William

Join my club and becum a n Outlaw

William Brown

You can join the Outlaws Club!
You will receive
✳ a special Outlaws wallet containing
your own Outlaws badge
the Club Rules
and
a letter from William giving you the secret password

To join the Club send a letter with your name and address written in block capitals telling us you want to join the Outlaws, and a postal order for 45p, to

The Outlaws Club
PO Box No 1
Gateshead
NE8 1AJ

You must live in the United Kingdom or the Republic of Ireland in order to join.

Chapter 1

William and the Musician

William sat on the crest of the hill, a small squat untidy figure, his chin cupped in his hands. From his point of vantage he surveyed the wide expanse of country that swept out before him, and as he surveyed it he became the owner of all the land and houses as far as he could see. Farther than he could see. Casting aside the hampering bonds of possibility as well as probability, he became the ruler of all England. Finding the confines even of England too cramping for him, he became the ruler of the whole world.

Assuming an air of sternness that bordered on ferocity, he made sweeping and imperious gestures with his right arm—gestures that sent his servants on missions to the farthest ends of the earth, that accorded praise or blame, that dealt out life or death, gestures at which the thousands of invisible minions around him trembled and sank to the ground, their foreheads in the dust. A rebellion was announced in a remote arm of his empire. With a wide movement of his arm, William sent out a vast army with instructions to show the rebels no quarter. Immediately afterwards the army returned, bringing with it in chains the leaders of the rebellion. A fierce movement of his arm ordered them off to instant execution. Another movement pinned medals on to the breasts of the victorious generals.

It was at this point that William realised that he was not alone. A small man had climbed the hill while William was engaged with his task of world-government, and now sat by him watching him with interest. Near the small man was a large pack.

"Well," he said pleasantly, as William turned to meet his eye, "did you catch it?"

"Catch what?" said William, taken aback.

"The mosquito you were trying to catch," said the little man. "I thought you got him that last grab."

William realised that his world-governing gestures had been interpreted as an attempt to catch a mosquito that was still hovering about him. Chagrined at this misconception, but unwilling to admit failure even with regard to mosquito-catching, he said coldly:

"Yes, I got him all right."

"You took a long time over it," said the man.

"Did I?" said William distantly.

Then, trying to recapture something of the glamour that the man's coming had so unceremoniously dispersed, he swept his arm around in another wide circle and added:

"All that land belongs to me. It's mine as far as you can see."

The man was evidently of a credulous and ingenuous disposition. He had a brown, humorous, pathetic face rather like a monkey's. He looked as impressed as ever William could have wished.

"All of it?" he said. "As far as you can see on every side?"

William had learnt that in dealing with ordinary limited human beings one's imagination should not be given too free a rein. He put the true artistic touch of restraint into his picture.

"Not *quite* as far as you can see," he said. "As far as that tree on one side, and as far as the river on the other."

The little man surveyed this extensive stretch of land with deepening interest. Then he looked at William.

"But—you're under age, of course. I suppose that you have a guardian or an agent of some sort to manage it for you."

"Oh yes," said William, reluctantly conceding the guardian or agent, "oh yes, I have a guardian or agent all right."

The little man was still credulous and impressed.

"Your parents are both dead, of course?" he said.

"Oh yes," said William disposing of his parents with unfilial promptitude. "Oh yes, my parents are both dead all right." And his love of the dramatic prompted him to add: "They died the day I was born. Struck by lightning."

"How terrible!" said the little man.

"Yes, it was," said William with well-assumed mournfulness. "I was awfully upset at the time, but"— his natural cheerfulness reasserting itself—"I soon got over it, and on the whole I'd as soon not have parents as have 'em."

In imagination he saw a glorious existence, untrammelled and unchecked, in which he climbed forbidden trees, played in forbidden ponds, turned the garden into a jungle and the house into a Red Indian camp, and never went to bed at all. "A jolly sight sooner, in fact," he ended with feeling.

The little man's gaze wandered again over the expanse of William's alleged estate.

"And where do you live?" he said.

The most imposing house within sight was the Hall—a palatial mansion with an impressive array of chimneys, surrounded by trees that clearly indicated a park and garden of the stately home of England type.

William pointed to it.

"I live there," he said.

As a matter of fact the Hall was rather in the public eye at present as Mr. Bott of Bott's Sauce fame had returned there with his wife and family after a long absence. Lest their return should pass unnoticed Mrs. Bott had given a staggering subscription to the rebuilding of Marleigh Cottage Hospital. The result of this was that the chairman of the hospital, Lord Faversham, was coming down from London to attend a party at the Hall, to which the entire neighbourhood was being invited and which was to assure for ever Mrs. Bott's place among the neighbouring aristocracy. William's thoughts went to the projected party. He had heard nothing else mentioned in the village for days past.

"I'm giving a large party there next Friday," he said nonchalantly. "Lord Faversham's coming to it."

He had checked an impulse to substitute "the King" for Lord Faversham's name, but could not resist adding: "and a lot more dukes and earls and things."

He did not watch his new friend's reaction to this, as he had suddenly caught sight of a little dog lying on the ground behind the pack, fast asleep.

His manner of landowner and world potentate vanished abruptly.

"I say," he said excitedly, "is that your dog?"

"Yes," said the little man, "it's Toby. Wake up, Toby. Show the gentleman what you can do, Toby."

Toby woke up and showed the gentleman what he

could do. He could walk on his hind legs and dance and shoulder a stick and pace up and down like a sentry. William watched him ecstatically.

"I say!" he gasped, "he's—he's *splendid*. I've never *seen*—Jumble can dance but only when someone holds his front paws—I've never *seen* such a clever dog!"

It was the first time that William had ever admitted to anyone that the world held a cleverer dog than Jumble. "Hi, Toby! Toby! Come here, old chap!"

Toby was nothing loth. He was a jolly, friendly little

"I SAY!" GASPED WILLIAM, "I'VE NEVER *SEEN* SUCH A CLEVER DOG!"

dog. He ran up to William and played with him and growled at him and pretended to bite him and rolled over and over, and then at the word of command sprang up to shoulder his stick and walk about with it.

"Never was such a dog," said the little man, watching his pet with gloomy tenderness. "Laps up tricks like a cat milk. But do people want him? No. Punch and Judy's out of date, they say. No use for him. No use for a Punch and Judy show nowadays. I don't know what the world's coming to."

William's eyes opened still further with eagerness.

"You got a Punch and Judy show?" he said.

The man nodded and pointed to his pack on which the faded letters "Signor Manelli" could faintly be descried. "Yes," he said. "Same as my father had before me, though my father never had a dog like Toby. Fine thing when a dog like Toby's told he's out of date and nobody wants to see him."

"I bet *anyone'd* want to see him," said William fervently.

The little man shook his head sadly but warmed to William's sympathy and became confidential.

He was an Italian, he said, and had come to England with his father and mother when he was only a few weeks old. He had never been out of England since, but his ambition was to make enough money to go back to Italy to his father's people. It was an ambition, however, that he had almost given up hopes of fulfilling.

"Turn up their noses at them nowadays, they do," he said disconsolately, "and a fine dog like Toby! It was different in my father's time. Hardly enough to keep us alive is all we get nowadays, me and Toby. And often enough we go hungry, don't we, Toby? Though it's share and share alike when there's anything at all."

"Well, I *like* Punch and Judy," said William stoutly, "and if——"

The little man interrupted him, his soft, brown, monkey-like eyes shining.

"Listen," he burst out, "this party you're giving on Friday. Couldn't you engage us for that? I promise that we'd give you our best performance. Your guests would not be disappointed."

A sudden blank look had come into William's face.

"Er—yes," he said flatly, "yes, of course."

"I'll come then?" said the little man eagerly, "what time does the party begin?"

"Er—three o'clock," said William, struggling with a nightmarish feeling of horror. "But I'm afraid—you see—I mean——"

The little man waved aside his feeble protest.

"I promise you I won't disappoint your guests. You won't regret it. I promise you. I thank you from my heart."

He had leapt to his feet and was already shouldering his pack. His eyes were bright with pleasure.

"Three o'clock on Friday," he said. "I'll not disappoint you. And we'll practise in the meantime till we're fit to perform before the King, won't we, Toby?"

Already he was swinging down the hill.

"But—look here—I say—wait a minute——" William called after him desperately.

The little man was already out of sight and earshot.

The world potentate sat with his head in his hands, gazing down into the valley and wondering how to deal with this new staggering crisis. The more he considered the situation, the more pregnant with horrible possibilities it became. Visions of his new friend's arriving at Mrs. Bott's party with his Punch and Judy show only to be ignominiously ejected, sent hot and cold tremors up and down his spine. Further visions of his new friend's appealing to him for protection, pointing to him as the author of his invitation, made the sweat break out on the world potentate's brow. The only possible way out of the difficulty was to run after the little man at once and make a clean breast of the whole thing. Having come to this conclusion, William set off hastily down the hill to the main road. There he stood looking up and down. There was no sign of anyone. Only, disappearing in the distance, was a 'bus, on the top of which William could just discern the small, bowed figure of his friend. In a vague desire to do all that was humanly possible, he ran down the road shouting and gesticulating till he could shout and gesticulate no longer. Then he sank down by the roadside and gave himself up again to gloomy reverie.

During the next few days he lived in a double nightmare, of which the subject was sometimes the little man arriving full of hope and pride at the Hall on Friday and being summarily dismissed by an enraged Mr. Bott, and sometimes himself on whom the hand of retribution would most surely fall. It would have been impossible for him to forget Friday in any case, as it was still being discussed on all sides.

"They're going to have an entertainment," his mother said at breakfast one morning.

"What sort of an entertainment?" said William hopefully. He thought that if no actual entertainment had been decided on he might perhaps call on Mr. Bott and recommend his friend.

"Zevrier, the violinist," said Mrs. Brown in an awestruck voice. "He's really *famous*, you know. And *terribly* modern."

"I wonder if—" said William tentatively, "I mean—well, I mean I know a man who—don't you think people would rather have a Punch and Judy show than a violinist?"

"A Punch and Judy show," repeated Mrs. Brown. "Don't be so *ridiculous*, William. It's not a children's party."

Her tone showed William the uselessness of pursuing the subject and he sighed deeply as he returned to his porridge, destroying in his absentmindedness a desert island that he had just made, on which a crystal of brown sugar represented a shipwrecked mariner scanning the sea of milk around him in hopes of a sail.

*   *   *

By the time Friday actually arrived, however, William's natural optimism had reasserted itself. The little man had, of course, taken the whole thing as a joke and would never think of it again. Still—he couldn't help occasionally remembering that gentle, ingenuous, monkey-like face. He didn't look the sort of man who took things as jokes. As William wandered about among the guests who were being marshalled by a perspiring Mrs. Bott, he kept an anxious eye upon the entrance gates. As the moments passed by, and no Signor Manelli appeared, his spirits lightened, and he began to take an interest in his surroundings. Lord Faversham, a tall, thin man wearing an expression of acute boredom, was being ushered by Mrs. Bott into the tent where Zevrier's recital was to take place.

Mrs. Bott had considered it a stroke of genius to have secured Zevrier.

"The swells like that sort of thing," she had explained

to her husband. "They don't like real music with a chune."

The expression of boredom on his Lordship's face intensified almost to agony as Mrs. Bott led him to the gothic armchair in the middle of the front row that marked his aristocratic status. Then Mrs. Bott went to the door to look up and down anxiously for Zevrier. The tentful of people began to grow restive. It was quarter-past three, and still there were no signs of Zevrier. The audience didn't particularly want to hear Zevrier, but it had come to hear him and it wanted to get it over.

Mrs. Bott, whose large, perspiring face now rivalled in colour her husband's famous sauce, went into the library, where her husband had sought temporary refuge in order to fortify himself with a stiff whisky and soda.

"Botty, he's not come," she said hysterically.

"Who's not come?" said Mr. Bott gloomily.

"Zebra, the violin man. Oh, Botty, what shall I do? They'll all be laughing at me. That there lord will go back to London laughing at me. I'll never hold up my head again. Oh, Botty, isn't it *awful*!"

Mr. Bott shook his head still more gloomily. Mr. Bott was a man completely given over to the manufacture of sauce and void of social ambitions. He had dreaded this affair for months, and it was proving worse than his worst fears.

"I can't help it," he said. "You *would* have all this set-out. I warned you it wouldn't come to no good."

"But Botty," she said still more hysterically, "there they are all waiting an' nothing happening and all getting so cranky! Can't you *do* something, Botty?"

"What can I do?" he said helplessly. "I can't play the vi'lin."

"No, but—Oh dear, oh dear, I'll go and see what's

happening now."

Meanwhile William, still urged by a nagging sense of anxiety and apprehension despite his determined optimism, had wandered down to the front gate in order to gaze once more up and down the road. To his relief there was no one in sight.

He wandered back to the tent. A little crowd of indignant figures had left their chairs and congregated round the tent door.

"*Really!*" they were saying. "Well—*really!*"

"One might have expected this sort of thing."

"How much longer does she think we're going to wait?"

At this point William turned round and saw a small, pack-laden figure approaching. His heart froze within him as the figure came up to him, gesticulating vehemently.

"Ah, my little host, I am so sorry to be so late. I came straight through the kitchen garden from the road so as to save time. The 'bus on which I was coming broke down. That is what has made me so late. I had to wait for another. Ah, here are your guests all ready for me. I will waste no more time. . . ."

Still speaking, he entered the tent, mounted the little platform that had been prepared for Zevrier, and began to set up his miniature stage.

William stood for a moment rooted to the ground by sheer horror, then, his courage suddenly failing him, began to run down the drive and along the road that led to his home.

He knew of a good place of concealment behind some bags of hop manure in his tool shed, where he could lie hidden and watch the course of events when his family returned. But just as he was rounding the corner of the boundaries of the Hall estate, he ran into a strange figure—a figure wearing an open collar, flowing tie, and a shock of long, carefully waved hair. It carried a violin-case. There was no doubt at all—it was Zevrier. William was going to hasten past when he noticed the musician's expression—ill-tempered, querulous. He remembered the appealing, rather helpless, friendliness of the little Punch and Judy man. He imagined the inevitable clash between them—the fury of the musician, the public humiliation of his little friend. Again the nightmare closed over him.

"Er—please," he began incoherently.

The musician stopped short and scowled at him.

"Yes?" he said.

"Er—are you going to the Hall?" asked William.

"Yes," snapped the musician.

"To play to them?"

"Yes."

"Are you Mr. Zevrier?"

"I'm Zevrier," said the man, tossing back his hair and striking an attitude.

"Well—well—I wouldn't go to play to them if I was you," said William desperately.

"Why not?" snapped the musician.

William silently considered this question. Should he say that Mrs. Bott had suddenly developed small-pox or that Mr. Bott had suddenly gone mad? There was something vaguely unconvincing about both statements.

"Well, I wouldn't," he finally said mysteriously, "if I was you. That's all."

The musician was feeling particularly annoyed that afternoon. He was engaged in writing his autobiography, and he could not find anything interesting to put into it. He wanted it to abound in picturesque episodes,

"I WOULDN'T GO TO PLAY TO THEM IF I WAS YOU," SAID WILLIAM
DESPERATELY.

and he couldn't find even one picturesque episode to put
into it. He had made his reputation for genius by defying
the established rules of technique, and he had an uneasy
suspicion that it was beginning to collapse. He was
writing the autobiography in order to bolster it up.
Moreover, he disliked Mrs. Bott, though he had never

met her. She was under a misapprehension about his name and began all her letters to him "Dear Mr. Zebra." This—and the frequency of the letters—had annoyed him so much that he had almost decided not to come and was still in two minds about it.

"Pigs!" he burst out suddenly without waiting for William's answer. "Buying immortal genius by the hour as if it were tape at so much a yard."

"Yes," said William, anxious to prolong the conversation. "Yes, that's just what I think about it."

"*You!*" said the musician glaring at him. "How can *you* understand?"

"I *do* understand," said William fervently. "I—well, I do understand. I mean, you tell me a bit more what you feel about it. I—I mean, I want to *know* what you feel about it."

William's attitude was that every word postponed the inevitable moment of reckoning.

"You—you don't know what music is to me," said the musician beating his chest dramatically.

"Yes, I do," said William solely for the sake of argument. Experience had taught him that with a little care and skill any argument can be prolonged almost indefinitely.

"*You* don't love music," said the musician.

"Yes, I do."

"It isn't—life and breath to you."

"Yes, it is."

The musician looked at William closely. William's expression was guileless and innocent. He could not know, of course, that William was probably the most unmusical boy in the British Empire.

He remembered an anecdote he had once heard about some musician or other—he'd forgotten which one. The

musician, on his way to play at a party, met a child lover
of music, and played to him all the afternoon, completely forgetting the party. So far as he knew, it had
never appeared in print, and it was just the sort of
anecdote that he wanted for his memoirs. It was, he felt,
rather kind of Fate to throw it in his way now. A
different type of boy went better with the anecdote in his
imagination, but he reflected that a little poetic licence in
descriptions is always allowed to writers of auto-
biographies.

"Those pigs will talk—talk while I play," said the
musician, waving his violin-case in the direction of the
Hall.

William saw the trend of this remark and said glibly:

"Yes, they will. They do all the time. The last man
that played to them couldn't hear what he was playing
for the noise they made. Well, I jolly well wouldn't play
to them if I was you."

"Suppose," said the musician, tossing back his long
hair, "suppose I played to you instead, would it be
something that you'd remember all your life?"

"Yes," said William, fixing an idiotic smile upon his
lips.

"I will," said the musician again, tossing back his long
hair and already beginning to compose the anecdote—
with picturesque additions—in his mind. "Let us go——"
His gaze roved round the landscape till it rested on a
haystack in a field next the road. That would look well in
a book of memoirs. Perhaps some artist would even be
inspired to paint the scene. With an idealised boy, of
course.

"Let us go there."

Arrived at the haystack, he sat down in the shade of it
with William next him and drew out his violin.

He played for quarter of an hour. Then he looked at William. William sat with a look of rapt attention on his face. The musician could not know, of course, that in sheer boredom William had returned to his *rôle* of world potentate, and was engaged in addressing his army on the eve of a great battle. He played again, then again he looked at William.

"Another one," said William in a peremptory tone of voice that the musician took to be one of fervent appreciation.

He could not know, of course, that William was now a pirate and was ordering his men to send yet another captured mariner along the plank.

He played again, then again looked at William.

William's eyes were closed as if in ecstasy. He could not know, of course, that William was asleep. He played again. The clock struck six. William sat up and heaved a sigh of relief.

"I've got to go home now," said William. "It's after my tea-time."

The musician glanced at him coldly and decided that the boy should make quite a different sort of remark in his memoirs.

They went back to the road in silence and there parted—William to his home and the musician to the station.

*   *   *

Mrs. Bott, still purple-faced and now on the verge of hysterics, went out to the hall where her lugubrious butler (he'd never got over having come down to trade) was standing and gazing gloomily at his boots whose radiance seemed to increase his dejection.

"Mr. Zebra hasn't come yet, Jenkins, has he?" said

Mrs. Bott hysterically.

"No, madam, I believe not," said the butler.

"It's horrible," moaned Mrs. Bott. "Between you and I, Jenkins, I believe he's let me down on purpose, I do reelly. You don't *do* anything do you, Jenkins?"

"*Do* anything, madam?" said Jenkins.

"Sing or recite or do conjuring tricks or anything."

"No, madam," said Jenkins with dignity.

"Well, they've got to have *something* done for them. They can't sit there staring at the platform all afternoon. I could *cry*—I could reelly, Jenkins. I used to do a skirt dance very pretty when I was a girl, but I'm past it now. Well, the only thing for me to do is go to them and ask if any of them recite. It'll be the death of me, I'll never live it down not if I live to be a hundred. I could *kill* that Zebra."

"He may have come by now, madam," said Jenkins, melted by her distress into a slight semblance of humanity. "He may have come and gone straight to the tent."

"I'll go and see," said Mrs. Bott, "and—and if he hasn't I'll never hold up my head again. After all I've done for them hospitals to be let down by a man with a name like something out of the Zoo!"

She went slowly down to the tent. To her amazement a burst of loud laughter and clapping greeted her. She peeped in at the open flap. Still more to her amazement a Punch and Judy stage was set upon the platform, and a Punch and Judy performance was in full and merry swing.

"I'm dreaming," she said. "Where's Zebra? Where did this thing come from? I *must* be dreaming."

Her eyes went to the noble lord. His air of languor had left him. He was leaning forward in his seat, laughing uproariously. After the first moment's stupefaction everyone else had settled down to follow his example and enjoy the show. Signor Manelli was a born comedian. Toby had a fine appreciation of the ludicrous and liked applause as much as his master. He carried his little sword with a swagger. Ever and anon he cocked a roguish eye at his audience. The whole thing was a relief to nerves keyed up to an hour's intensive torture at the hands of a Zevrier.

"What's happened?" murmured Mrs. Bott wildly. Then, as if coming to the only possible conclusion, she added resignedly: "I've gone potty. That's what's happened. This whole set-out's been too much for my brain, and I've gone potty."

But the performance was drawing to a close amid a riot of applause. The noble lord had mounted the platform, and was shaking Signor Manelli by the hand.

"Bravo!" he was saying, "I've not enjoyed anything so much for years. Not for *years*. Now, look here, I want to book you for a party at my place in town next month. Have you a free date?"

It appeared that Signor Manelli had a free date.

Arrangements were quickly made. A fee was named at which Signor Manelli almost fainted in sheer surprise. Suddenly the noble lord saw Mrs. Bott standing in the doorway of the tent, the expression of surprise upon her face making it strongly resemble that of expiring fish.

"Ah!" he said genially, "here is our hostess to whom we owe this delightful entertainment."

Signor Manelli started forward to her eagerly.

"And where," he said, "is my little host?"

The mystery was suddenly clear to Mrs. Bott. Botty in the kindness of his heart must have engaged this man for her to fall back on in case the Zebra person didn't turn up. He hadn't mentioned it to her, but it was just like

Botty to do a thoughtful thing like that and not mention it. He loved giving her little surprises. "My little host" was a bit of cheek, of course, but there wasn't any denying that Botty's stoutness made him seem even shorter than he was; and it was a well-known fact that foreigners hadn't any manners, poor things. Look at that Zebra person never turning up in spite of her having reminded him by every post for weeks. . . .

"He's resting in the library," she said.

"I won't disturb him then," said Signor Manelli, "but give the dear little man my most grateful respects and tell him that I shall never forget his kindness to me."

"Yes, I'll tell him," said Mrs. Bott, and was at once surrounded by an eager crowd congratulating her on the success of her entertainment.

"He's a genius. How *did* you find him?"

"I've never laughed so much for ages."

"It was so *daring* of you. I'd never have *dared* to do it."

"I'm going to try to get him for my garden party."

"I'd heard that it was going to be Zevrier, and he's so frightfully, frightfully modern that, to be quite frank, I was *dreading* it."

"Of course, the world's just ready for a revival of the Punch and Judy show. It's so *clever* of you to hit the exact *moment*, Mrs. Bott."

To her amazement Mrs. Bott discovered that her party had been a roaring success and that she was at last "somebody".

When her guests had departed, she sought out her husband, who was still "resting" in the library.

"Oh, Botty," she said hysterically, "how kind, how thoughtful of you to think of it. I shall never forget it—never."

He laid his hand gently on her shoulder.

"You go and lie down, my dear," he said, "the excitement's gone to your head."

The Browns were walking slowly homeward.

ARRANGEMENTS WERE QUICKLY MADE, AND A FEE WAS NAMED AT WHICH MANELLI ALMOST FAINTED IN SURPRISE.

"I didn't see William there after the beginning, did you?" said Ethel.

"He must have been there somewhere," said Mrs. Brown. "I'm sure he loved the Punch and Judy show."

*　　*　　*

It was several months later. William sat at the table, ostensibly engaged upon his homework. Mrs. Brown was reading the paper and keeping up a desultory

SUDDENLY MRS. BOTT STOOD IN THE DOORWAY OF THE TENT, AN EXPRESSION OF WONDER ON HER FACE.

conversation with Ethel, who was embroidering a
nightgown.

"It says that Punch and Judy is still all the rage in
London," said Mrs. Brown, adjusting her spectacles,
"but that Signor Manelli who started it is making no
more engagements, because he's going back to Italy. Do
you remember him, dear? We saw him at that party of
Mrs. Bott's."

"Yes," said Ethel, comparing sewing silks with a
critical frown.

"And here's something about that Mr. Zevrier, the
musician that Mrs. Bott once thought of having to her
party, you know, before she decided to have the Punch
and Judy. . . ."

"What?" said Ethel absently.

"His book of memoirs has just been published. And it
quotes an extract from it here. All about a musical child
that he met when he was going to play at some sort of
party and he stayed playing to it and forgot the party and
his fee and everything." She looked up. "I wonder—I
wonder if it could possibly have been—you know,
people said that Mrs. Bott had engaged him for her party
as well as the Punch and Judy show and he didn't turn
up. Could it have been *here* that he met this musical
child?"

"What sort of a child was it?" said Ethel.

"It quotes the description from the book," said Mrs.
Brown. "Here it is: 'He had deep-set, dark eyes and a
pale, oval face, sensitive lips, and dark curly hair. I saw
at once that to him as to me music was the very breath of
life.'"

Ethel laughed shortly.

"No, it couldn't have been here," she said. "There
isn't any child like *that* about here."

His head bent over the Chief Dates of the Wars of the Roses and shielded by his hands in the attitude of one who wishes to devote himself entirely to study and shut out all disturbing influences, William grinned to himself. . . .

Chapter 2

William Holds the Stage

It was an old boy of William's school, called Mr. Welbecker, who with well-intentioned but mistaken enthusiasm offered a prize to the form that should act a scene from Shakespeare most successfully. The old boy in question had written an article on Shakespeare which had appeared in the columns of the local press, and, being a man of more means than discernment, thought it well to commemorate his intellectual achievement and immortalise his name by instituting the Welbecker Shakespeare Acting Shield in his old school.

The headmaster and the staff received his offer with conventional gratitude but without enthusiasm. Several of the senior members of the staff were heard to express a wish that that fool Welbecker could have the trouble of organising the thing himself, adding that he jolly well wouldn't do it more than once. The junior staff expressed all this more simply and forcibly by saying that the blighter ought to be hanged. To make matters worse, the blighter arrived at the school one morning, unheralded and unexpected, armed with innumerable copies of his article on Shakespeare, privately printed and bound in white vellum with gold lettering, and, after distributing them broadcast, offered to give a lecture on

Shakespeare to the school. The headmaster hastily said that it was impossible to arrange for him to give a lecture to the school. He said politely and unblushingly that he was sure that it would be a deep disappointment to the boys, but that the routine of the school would not allow of it on that particular day. The author offered to come another time when arrangements could be made beforehand. The headmaster replied evasively that he would see about it.

It was at this moment that the second master came in to ask what was to be done about IIIa, explaining that the master who should be teaching it had suddenly been taken ill. He implied in discreet, well-chosen words that IIIa was engaged in raising Cain in their form room and that no one within a mile of them could hear himself speak. The headmaster raised a hand to his head wearily, then his eye fell upon the Shakespearean author, and he brightened.

"Perhaps you'd give your lecture on Shakespeare to IIIa," he suggested suavely.

"It's young Brown and that set," murmured the second master warningly. The headmaster's expression brightened still further. So might a man look who was sending his bitterest enemy unarmed and unsuspecting into a lions' den.

"Splendid!" he said heartily, "splendid! I'm sure they'll find your lecture most interesting, Welbecker. *Good* morning. I hope to see you, of course, before you go."

A sudden silence—a silence of interest and surprise —greeted the entry of Mr. Welbecker into the classroom of IIIa.

"Now boys," he said breezily, "I want to give you a little talk about Shakespeare, and I want you to ask me

questions freely, because I'm—er—well, I'm what you
might call an expert on the subject. I've written a little
book, some copies of which I have with me now, and
which I'm going to give to the boys who seem to me to
show the most intelligence. I'm sure that they will always
be among your greatest treasures, because—well, it isn't
everyone who can write a book, you know, is it?"

"I've written a book," put in William nonchalantly.

"Perhaps," said Mr. Welbecker, smiling tolerantly,
"but you've not had it published, have you?"

"No," said William, "I've not tried to have it
published yet."

"And it wasn't on Shakespeare, was it?" said Mr.
Welbecker, smiling still more tolerantly.

"No," said William. "It was about someone a jolly
sight more int'restn' than Shakespeare. It was about a
pirate called Dick of the Bloody Hand, an' he started off
in search of adventure an' he came to——"

"Yes," said Mr. Welbecker hastily, "but I just want
to tell you a little about Shakespeare first. Now the
theory I incline to is that Bacon wrote the plays of
Shakespeare."

"I wrote a play once," said William, "and people
acted it, but they all forgot their parts, so it didn't come
to much, but it was a jolly fine play all the same."

"I wish you wouldn't keep interrupting," said Mr.
Welbecker testily.

"I thought you said we could ask questions," said
William.

"Yes, I did, but you're not asking questions."

"I know I'm not," said William, "but I don't see any
difference in asking a question and telling you something
int'restin'."

Most of the class had by now settled down to their own

"YOU SAID WE COULD ASK QUESTIONS," SAID
WILLIAM.

devices—quiet or otherwise. William was the only one
who seemed to be taking any interest in the lecture or the
lecturer. William, on the strength of his play and story,
considered himself a literary character, and was quite
willing to give a hearing to a brother artist.

"Well," said Mr. Welbecker, assuming his lecturer's
manner, gazing round at his audience, and returning at
last reluctantly to William, "I repeat that I incline to the
theory that the plays of Shakespeare were written by
Bacon."

"How could they be?" said William.

"I've already said that I wished you wouldn't keep
interrupting," snapped the lecturer.

"That *was* a question," said William triumphantly. "You can't say that wasn't a question, and you said we could ask questions. How could that other man Ham——"

"I said Bacon."

"Well, it's nearly the same," said William. "Well, how could this man Bacon write them if Shakespeare wrote them?"

"Ah, but you see I don't believe that Shakespeare did write them," said Mr. Welbecker mysteriously.

"Well, why's he got his name printed on all the books then?" said William. "He must've told the printers he did, or they wouldn't put his name on, an' he ought to know. An' if this other man Eggs——"

"I said Bacon," snapped Mr. Welbecker again.

"Well, Bacon, then," said William, "well, if this man Bacon wrote them, they wouldn't put this man Shakespeare's name on the books. They wouldn't be allowed to. They'd get put in prison for it. The only way he could have done it was by poisoning this man Shakespeare and then stealing his plays. That's what I'd have done, anyway, if I'd been him, and I'd wanted to say I'd written them."

"That's all nonsense," said Mr. Welbecker sharply. "Of course I'm willing to admit that it's an open question." Then, returning to his breezy manner and making an unsuccessful attempt to enlarge his audience: "Now, boys, I want you all please to listen to me——"

No one responded. Those who were playing noughts and crosses continued to play noughts and crosses. Those who were engaged in mimic battles, the ammunition of which consisted in pellets of blotting-paper soaked in ink, continued to be so engaged. Those who were playing that game of cricket in which a rubber represents the ball and a ruler the bat remained engrossed in it. The boy who was drawing low-pitched but irritating sounds from a whistle continued to draw low-pitched but irritating sounds from a whistle. Dejectedly Mr. Welbecker returned to his sole auditor.

"I want first to tell you the story of the play of which you are all going to act a scene for the shield that I am presenting," he said. "There was a man called Hamlet——"

"You just said he was called Bacon," said William.

"I did *not* say he was called Bacon," snapped Mr. Welbecker.

"Yes, 'scuse me, you did," said William politely. "When I called him Ham you said it was Bacon, and now you're calling him Ham yourself."

"This was a different man," said Mr. Welbecker. "*Listen!* This man was called Hamlet and his uncle had killed his father because he wanted to marry his mother."

"What did he want to marry his mother for?" said William. "I've never heard of anyone wanting to marry their mother."

"It was *Hamlet's* mother he wanted to marry."

"Oh, that man that you think wrote the plays."

"No, that was Bacon."

"You said it was Ham a minute ago. Whenever I say it's Bacon you say it's Ham, and whenever I say it's Ham you say it's Bacon. I don't think you know *which* his name was."

"Will you *listen!*" said the distraught lecturer. "This man Hamlet decided to kill his uncle."

"Why?"

"I've told you. Because his uncle had killed his father."

"Whose father?"

"*Hamlet's*. There's a beautiful girl in the play called Ophelia, and Hamlet had once wanted to marry her."

"You just said he wanted to marry his mother."

"I did *not*. I wish you'd listen. Then he went mad, and this girl fell into the river. It was supposed to be an accident, but probably——"

"He pushed her in," supplied William.

"*Who* pushed her?" demanded Mr. Welbecker irritably.

"I thought you were going to say that that man Bacon pushed her in."

"*Hamlet*, you mean."

"I tell you what," said William confidingly, "let's say Eggs for both of them. Then we shan't get so muddled. Eggs means whichever of them it was."

"Rubbish!" exploded the lecturer. "Listen—I'll begin all over again." But just at that minute the bell rang, and the headmaster entered the room. Immediately whistle, rubbers, rulers, noughts and crosses, pellets, vanished as by magic, and twenty-five earnest, attentive faces were turned towards the lecturer. So intent were they on the lecture that apparently they were unaware that the headmaster had entered the room, for not one turned in his direction.

"This is the end of the period, Welbecker," said the headmaster. "A thousand thanks for your help and your most interesting lecture. I'm sure you've enjoyed it tremendously, haven't you boys?"

A thunder of applause bore tribute to their enjoyment.

"Now," continued the headmaster rather maliciously, "I want one of you to give me a short account of Mr. Welbecker's lecture. Let any one of you who thinks he can do so put up his hand."

Only one hand went up, and it was William's.

"Well, Brown?" said the headmaster.

"Please, sir, he told us that he thinks that the plays of Shakespeare were really written by a man called Ham and that Shakespeare poisoned this man called Ham and stole the plays and then pretended he'd written them. And then a man called Bacon pushed a woman into a pond because he wanted to marry his mother. And there's a man called Eggs, but I've forgotten what he did except that——"

Mr. Welbecker's complexion had assumed a greenish hue.

"That will do, Brown," said the headmaster very quietly.

* * *

Despite this contretemps, the preparations for the Shakespeare acting competition continued apace. Mr. Welbecker had chosen Act III, Scene I, to be acted for the Shield. The parts of the Queen and Ophelia were to be played by boys, "as was the custom in Shakespeare's time," said Mr. Welbecker, who seemed to cherish a pathetic delusion that no one had ever known anything about Shakespeare before his article appeared in the local press.

"I'm not going to be the woman that gets pushed into a pond," said William firmly. "I don't mind being the one that pushes her, and I don't mind being the one called Ham that poisons Shakespeare. I don't much mind which of them I am so long as I'm not the one that gets pushed into a pond, and as long as I've got a lot to say. When I'm in a play I like to have a lot to say."

His interest in the play was increased by the fact that Dorinda Lane was once more staying at her aunt's in the village. Dorinda was a little girl with dark hair and dimples, who was the temporary possessor of William's heart, a hard-boiled organ that generally scorned thraldom to any woman. Dorinda, however, appeared on his horizon so seldom that, for the short duration of her visits, he could stoop from his heroic pinnacle of manliness to admire her without losing prestige in his own eyes.

"I'm goin' to be in a play at school," he informed her the morning after Mr. Welbecker's lecture.

She gave a little cry of excitement. Her admiration of William was absolute and unmixed.

"Oh, William!" she said, "how lovely! What are you going to be?"

"I'm not quite sure," said William, "but anyway I'm goin' to be the most important person in it."

"Oh, *are* you, William?"

"Yes. I'm going to be the one that poisons Bacon or that pushes Ham into a pond or something like that. Anyway, we had a lecture about it, and I was the only one that knew anything about it at the end, so they're going to give me the biggest part."

"Oh, William, how lovely! Have they told you so?"

William hesitated.

"Well, they've as good as told me," he said. "I mean, I was the only one that knew anything about it when they'd finished giving this lecture, so they're sure to give me the biggest part. In fact"—finally surrendering to his imagination—"in fact, they *told* me they were. They said: 'You seem to be the only one that knows anything about this man Eggs what wrote the play so you choose what you'd like to be in it.'"

"I'M GOING TO BE THE MOST IMPORTANT PERSON IN THE PLAY,"
SAID WILLIAM.

"Oh, William," said Dorinda, "I think you're wonderful."

After this William, convinced by his own eloquence, firmly believed that he was to be offered the best part in the scene, because of his masterly recapitulation of its plot. In order to be sure of making a good choice, he borrowed a Shakespeare from his father, turned to the scene (with much difficulty), and began to read it through. He found it as incomprehensible as if it had been written in a foreign language, but he was greatly struck by the speech beginning "To be or not to be——" It was long, it was even more incomprehensible than the rest of the scene, it went with a weirdly impressive swing. William loved speeches that were long and incomprehensible and that went with a swing. He mouthed it with infinite gusto and many gesticulations, striding to and fro in his bedroom. He decided quite finally that he would be Hamlet.

His surprise and disgust, therefore, were unbounded when his form master told him that he was to be one of the attendants on the king, and that, as such, he would not be required to say anything at all.

"You just go in first of all and stand by the throne and then go out when the king goes out."

"But I want to say something," protested William.

"I've no doubt you do," said his form master dryly. "I've never known you yet when you didn't. But as it happens, the attendant doesn't speak. By a strange oversight Shakespeare didn't write any lines for him."

"Well, I don't mind writin' some myself. I'll write it and learn it."

"If you learn it as well as you learnt your Latin verbs yesterday," said the form master sarcastically, "it'll be worth listening to."

"Well, I don't *like* Latin verbs," said William, "and I *do* like acting."

But it was in vain. His form master was adamant. He was to be one of the king's attendants and he was not to say anything. William's first plan was to feign illness on the day of the play and to tell Dorinda that a substitute had had to be hastily found for him but that he would have done the part much better. There were, however, obvious drawbacks to this course. For one thing he had never yet managed to feign illness with any success. His family doctor was a suspicious and, in William's eyes, inhuman being, who always drove William from his sickbed to whatever he was trying to avoid by draughts of nauseous medicine. ("It's better than bein' poisoned anyway," William would say bitterly, as he finally abandoned his symptoms.) Moreover, even if he succeeded in outwitting the doctor (a thing he had never done yet) the whole proceeding would be rather tame. If there was anything going on William liked to be in it.

It was a chance remark of his father's that sent a ray of light into the gloom of the situation.

It happened that this same play was being acted at a London theatre, and that the actor who should have played Hamlet had been taken ill and the part played by another member of the cast at the last minute.

"This other fellow knew the part," said his father, "so he stepped into the breach."

"Why did he do that?" said William.

"Do what?" asked his father.

"Step into that thing you said."

"What thing?"

"You just said he stepped into something."

"I said he played the part."

"Well, you said he stepped into somethin', an' I thought perhaps he broke it like Robert did steppin' into one of the footlights when he was acting in that play the football club did."

His father's only reply was a grunt that was obviously intended to close the conversation.

But William's way now lay clear before him. He would learn Hamlet's part, and on the night of the play, when Hamlet was taken ill, he would come forward to play the part for him. ("An' I won't go messin' about steppin' into things same as the one in London did," he said sternly.)

In William's eyes the part of Hamlet consisted solely of the "To be or not to be" speech. "If I learn that I'll be all right," he told himself. "I can jus' make up the rest. Jus' say what comes into my head when they say things to me."

Every night he repeated the speech before his looking-glass with eloquent and windmill-like gestures that swept everything off his dressing-table onto the floor in all directions.

As his head was the only part of his person that was visible in the looking-glass, he did not trouble to dress up more than his head for his part. Sometimes he clothed it Arab fashion in his towel, sometimes in his Red Indian head-dress, sometimes in his father's top hat, "borrowed" for the occasion. On the whole he thought that the top hat gave the best effect.

"Are you *really* going to be the hero, William?" said Dorinda when next she met him.

"Yes, I have a speech that takes hours and hours to say. The longest there's ever been in a play. I stand in the middle of stage, and I go on talkin' an' talkin' sayin' the things in this speech with no one stoppin' me, or interruptin' me. For *hours*. 'Cause I'm the person the whole play's written about."

"Oh, William, how lovely! What's the speech about?"

As William, though now able to repeat the speech almost perfectly, had not the faintest idea what it was about, he merely smiled mysteriously and said: "Oh, you'll have to wait and see."

"Is it funny, William? Will it make me laugh? I *love* funny things."

William considered. For all he knew the speech might be intended to be humorous. On the other hand, of course, it might not be. Having no key to its meaning, he could not tell.

"You'll have to wait and see," he said with the air of one to whom weighty state secrets are entrusted, and who is bound on honour not to betray them.

He had now abandoned his looking-glass as an audience, and strode to and fro uttering his speech with its ample accompaniment of gestures to an audience of his wash-stand and a chair and a photograph of his mother's and father's wedding group that had slowly descended the ladder of importance, working its way in the course of the years from the drawing-room to the dining-room, from the dining-room to the morning-room, from the morning-room to the hall, from the hall to the staircase, and then through his mother's, Robert's, and Ethel's bedrooms to the bottom rung of the ladder in William's. William, of course, did not see the wash-stand and the chair and the wedding group; he saw ranks upon serried ranks of intent faces, Dorinda's standing out from among them with startling clearness.

"To be or not to be," he would declaim, "that is the question, whether 'tis nobler in the slings to suffer

The mind and arrows of opposing fortune

Or to die to sleep against a sea of troubles.

And by opposing end there."

Even William did not pretend to get every word in its exact place. As he said to himself: "It's as sens'ble as what's in the book, anyway, and it sounds all right."

The subordinate part that he took in the rehearsals as
the king's attendant did not trouble him in the least. He
was not the king's attendant. He was Hamlet. He was
the tall, dark boy called Dalrymple (he had adenoids and
a slight lisp but excellent memory) who played Hamlet.
It was he, William, not Dalrymple, who repeated that
long and thrilling speech to an enthralled audience. So
entirely did William trust in his star that he had not the
slightest doubt that Dalrymple would develop some
illness on the day of the play. William's mother had an
enormous book with the title "Every-day Ailments."
William glanced through it idly and was much cheered
by it. There were so many illnesses that it seemed
impossible that Dalrymple—a mere mortal and susceptible to all the germs with which the air was apparently
laden—should not be stricken down by one or another of
them on the day of the play. Dorinda met him in the
village the day before the performance.

"I'm *longing* for to-morrow, William," she said.

And William, without the slightest qualm of doubt,
replied:

"Oh, yes, it'll be jolly fine. You look out for my long
speech."

The day of the performance dawned. No news of any
sudden illness of Dalrymple's reached William, yet he
still felt no doubts. His star had marked him out for
Hamlet, and Hamlet he would be. His mother, who was
anxious for him not to be late, saw him off for the
performance at what William considered an unduly
early hour with many admonitions not to loiter on the
way. She herself was coming later as part of the
audience. William had a strong dislike of arriving too
early at any objective. He considered that his mother
had made him set off quite a quarter of an hour too soon,

and therefore that he had a quarter of an hour to spend
on the way. He still felt no doubts that he would play the
part of Hamlet, but he was not narrow in his interests,
and he realised even at that moment that there were
other things in the world than Hamlet. There was the
stream in Crown Woods (he had decided to go the longer
way through Crown Woods in order to make up the
quarter of an hour), there was a hedge sparrow's nest,
there was a curious insect which William had never seen
before and of which he thought that he must be the first
discoverer, there was a path that William had not
noticed on his previous visits to the wood and that had
therefore to be explored, there was a tree whose
challenge to climb it William could not possibly resist.
Even William realised, on emerging from the wood, that
he had spent in it more than the quarter of an hour that
he considered his due.

He ran in the direction of the school. An excited group
of people was standing at the gate, looking out for him.
They received him with a stream of indignant
reproaches, bundled him into his form room and began
to pull off his clothes and hustle him into his attendant's
uniform. ("It's time to *begin*. We've been waiting for
you for *ages*. Why on *earth* couldn't you get here in
time?") All the others had changed and were ready in
their costumes. Hamlet looked picturesque in black
velvet slashed with purple, wearing a silver chain.
William tried to collect his forces, but his legs were being
thrust into tights by one person, his hair was being
mercilessly brushed by another, and his face was being
made up by another. Whenever he opened his mouth to
speak, it received a stick of make-up or an eyebrow
pencil or a hare's foot.

"Now don't forget," said the form master, who was

also the producer, "you go on first of all and stand by the throne. Stand quite stiffly, as I showed you, and in a few moments the king and the others will come on."

And William, his faculties still in a whirl, was thrust unceremoniously upon the empty stage.

"COME *OFF*, I TELL YOU," REPEATED THE FORM MASTER
FRANTICALLY.

He stood there facing a sea of upturned, intent faces. Among them in the second row he discerned that of Dorinda, her eyes fixed expectantly upon him.

Instinctively and without a moment's hesitation, he stepped forward and with a sweeping gesture launched into his speech:

WILLIAM WAS UNAWARE OF THE FROZEN FACES OF THE HEADMASTER AND OF MR. WELBECKER, WHO SAT IN THE FRONT ROW.

"To be or not to be that is the question
Whether 'tis nobler in the mind to suffer——"

"Come off, you young fool," hissed the form master wildly from behind the scenes.

But William had got well into his stride and was not coming off for anyone.

"The stings and arrows of outrageous fortune." (For a wonder he was getting the words in their right places.)

"Or to take arms against a sea of troubles."

The best thing, of course, would have been to lower the curtain, but there was no curtain to lower.

Screens had been set along the edge of the stage and had been folded up when the performance was to begin.

"Come *off*, I tell you," repeated the form master frantically.

"And by opposing end there. To sleep to die."

William had forgotten everything in the world but himself, his words, and Dorinda. He was unaware of the crowd of distraught players hissing and gesticulating off the stage; he was unaware of his form master's frenzied commands, of the frozen faces of the headmaster and Mr. Welbecker, who sat holding his shield ready for presentation in the front row.

"No more and by a sleep to say an end."

The form master decided to act. The boy had evidently gone mad. The only thing to do was to go boldly onto the stage and drag him off. This the form master attempted to do. He stalked onto the stage and put out his hand to seize William. William, vaguely aware that someone was trying to stop him saying his speech, reacted promptly, and dodged to the other side of the stage, still continuing his recital.

"The thousand natural shocks the flesh and hair is."

The form master, whose blood was now up, plunged

across the stage. Once more William dodged his outstretched hand, and, still breathlessly reciting, reached the other end of the stage again. Then followed the diverting spectacle of the form master chasing William round the stage—William dodging, doubling, and all the time continuing his speech. Someone had the timely idea of trying to set up the screens again, but it was a manœuvre that defeated its own ends, for William (still reciting) merely dodged round and behind them and unfortunately one of them fell down on the top of the form master. A mighty roar ascended from the audience. Dorinda was rocking to and fro with mirth and clapping with all her might and main. The unseemly performance came to an end at last. The players joined the form master in the chase, and William, still reciting, was dragged ingloriously from the stage.

Mr. Welbecker turned a purple face to the head-master.

"This is an outrage," he said; "an insult. I should not dream of presenting my shield to a school in which I have seen this exhibition."

"I agree that it's a most regrettable incident, Welbecker," said the headmaster suavely, "and I think that in the circumstances your decision is amply justified."

Dorinda was wiping tears of laughter from her eyes.

"Wasn't William *wonderful*?" she said.

* * *

It was, of course, felt by the staff of William's school that someone ought to deal drastically with William, but it was so difficult not to regard him as a public benefactor (for the thought of the annual Welbecker Shield

Shakespeare Competition had begun to assume the proportion of a nightmare in the minds of an already overworked staff) that no definite move had been taken in the matter beyond the rough and (very) ready primitive measures meted out on the spot by the form master.

School had broken up the next day, and, when it had quite safely broken up, the headmaster and form master informed each other just for the look of the thing that each thought the other was dealing officially with William.

"It was unpardonable," said the headmaster, "but it's too late to do anything now that the term's over. I'll send for him at the beginning of next term."

"That will be best," said the form master, who was quite sure that he would forget.

Mrs. Brown had crept out of the hall at the beginning of the incident and was pretending to herself and everyone else that she had not gone to the performance at all, and so knew nothing about it.

A fortnight after the end of term William went to tea with Dorinda—a magnificent cross-country journey involving a train ride and two 'bus rides. Dorinda's mother supplied a sumptuous tea, and William, watched admiringly by Dorinda, did full justice to it.

"Dorinda so much enjoyed that play at your school, William," said Dorinda's mother, watching the rapid disappearance of an iced cake with dispassionate wonder. "She said when she came home that she never laughed so much in all her life. She couldn't remember much of the plot but she said it was awfully funny. It was a farce, wasn't it?"

"Yes," said William, unwilling to admit that he did not know what the word farce meant.

"What was it called? We used to act a lot of farces when I was young."

William gazed frowningly into the distance.

"I've forgotten," he said, then his face cleared. "Oh yes, I remember. It was called 'Eggs and Bacon'."

Chapter 3

The Outlaws and the Triplets

William's aunt's invitation was looked upon by William's family as little short of providential. The Browns had decided not to go away that summer. They had decided that a holiday at home would be a pleasant change. The only drawback would be the presence of William. The presence of William was not compatible with that atmosphere of peace that is so necessary to a perfect holiday.

"Wouldn't it be *heavenly*," said William's sister, Ethel, "if someone would ask William somewhere for even a week? For next week specially."

And she thought of the tennis party she had arranged to give the next week. She imagined the blissful feeling of security that William's absence would lend to it and compared it with her present feeling of gloomy certainty that everything was sure to go wrong. William, even when inspired by the best motives, seemed invariably to wreck every function which he attended, and he naturally expected to attend those held by his own family on their own premises. He was already deeply interested in the prospect of Ethel's tennis party.

"I'll think out some new sorts of games, Ethel," he had volunteered, "somethin' that'll make it go with a bit of a swing. I bet everyone's tired of tennis. I bet I can find somethin' more excitin' than that ole game."

Ethel forbade him vehemently to meddle in her party. "All I want you to do," she told him sternly, "is to keep out of the way."

He said: "All right," meekly enough, but she had an uneasy suspicion that he was planning some surprise.

Mrs. Brown, loyal to all her children even in the most trying circumstances, refused openly to admit the undesirability of William's presence.

"I'm sure that he'll be good, dear," she said to Ethel. "I'm certain he'll do his very best not to be a nuisance. But still," she ended meditatively, "it *would* be rather nice if Aunt Jane asked him to stay with her for a week or so. She's often said that she would."

Great, therefore, was the jubilation in William's family when the invitation actually arrived. Then the jubilation died away. William refused to go. He said that he didn't want to miss Ethel's party. He was hurt and amazed by the general attitude.

"Well, *why* d'you want me to go?" he said. "I should've thought this was just the time you *wouldn't* want me to go. I should've thought you'd all wanted me to stay and help with Ethel's party. . . . *Me* upset things? *Course* I won't upset things. I keep *tellin'* you I'm goin' to *help*. Well, I don't care what sort of a good time Aunt Jane would give me, I don't want to miss Ethel's party. I don't *like* Aunt Jane, anyway. She kept askin' me history dates the last time I saw her. I'd much rather stay an' help Ethel with her party."

He was adamant. It was impossible to send him away against his will. He didn't *want* to go to stay with Aunt Jane. He wanted to stay and help Ethel with her party.

His family spent hours of useless labour arguing with

him. They pointed out the benefits that would accrue to
him in the way of health and fresh interests from the
change. He refused to be moved from his position. He
didn't want to go to stay with Aunt Jane (he repeated *ad
nauseam* that she had asked him history dates the last
time he had seen her) and he did want to stay and help
Ethel with her party.

In the end his family, worn out by argument, surrendered, and Mrs. Brown wrote to Aunt Jane a letter of
such consummate tact that Aunt Jane replied saying that
she thought it just a little selfish of dear Ethel to insist on
William's staying at home so that he could help her with
the preparations for her party, but that she would expect
dear William as soon as Ethel could manage without
him, and all they would have to do would be to send a
wire, and would Mrs. Brown give dear William her love
and tell him that she would have known how much he
longed to see her even without his dear mother's telling
her.

Gloomily, therefore, Ethel surrendered to Fate. William was amused by her attitude.

"Wait till the time comes," he said; "you'll be *jolly*
glad I didn't go away. There'll never have *been* such a
party."

This ominous prophecy did not lessen Ethel's fore-
boding, and her dejection increased as the day of the
party approached. She watched William with morbid
interest.

"Are there any infectious diseases he hasn't had,
mother?" she asked, a far-away hope springing up in her
breast.

"Not many," said his mother, and understanding the
trend of Ethel's question, added: "If he got anything,
you know, dear, we'd all have to be in quarantine."

The faint, far-away hope died down in Ethel's breast.

It so happened that William had formed no actual plans for enlivening the party. He merely considered it his duty to get a little more "go" into it than there had been in her last one—a very dull affair, he considered, in which the guests had merely played tennis or sat about and talked.

He was on his way to meet his Outlaws now, and he meant to discuss the situation with them fully.

They were waiting for him in the road outside Henry's house—all but Henry, whose voice was heard within the garden raised in passionate altercation with his mother.

"Well, why must I? Why can't someone else take it out?"

"I keep *telling* you, dear. There's no one else to take her out. Nannie's gone to bed with a headache, and I can't leave the house."

"Why can't she stay in the garden?" said Henry.

"She's been in the garden all morning and she's tired of it. She won't be any trouble. You ought to *like* taking out your little sister in her pram, Henry. You ought to be *proud* of her."

"Well, I'm jolly well not," retorted Henry. "I'm *sick* of her—pulling my hair and taking all my things and getting me into rows by yelling if ever I try to do anything back."

"*Henry!*"—the voice was deeply shocked. "How *can* you talk like that! There never was such a sweet baby. Hundreds of little boys would give anything to have her for a sister."

"I wish they could have her then, that's all," said Henry bitterly. "Oh, all right, I'll take her."

"That's a good boy. Keep her out about half an hour. And remember to call at the grocer's for the tea."

Walking slowly and gloomily, Henry came down the garden path, pushing a pram.

His three friends surveyed him without enthusiasm.

"She made me bring it," he said. "An' I've got to go to the grocer's. Well, you needn't come with me if you don't want."

But the Outlaws, though acutely sensible of the ignominy of the proceeding, did not intend to forsake him.

"Oh, we'll come all right," said William, "but anyone with a bit of *sense* would have got out of it somehow. Why din't you say you'd hurt your wrist?"

"'Cause she knows I haven't," answered Henry simply.

"Well, why din't you say you felt too ill?"

"'Cause I'd rather come out an' push a pram than go to bed. An' I've told you you needn't come if you don't want to."

They walked along the road in a somewhat gloomy silence. It was difficult to sustain their usual characters of brigands or pirates in the face of Henry's pram.

It was William's idea to pretend that it was a gun-carriage and that they were hastening with it to the relief of a beleaguered army. They pushed it in turns and ran with it at a quick trot.

Its occupant seemed to find the movement soporific and was fast asleep by the time they reached the grocer's. Ginger had had twopence given him by his mother for rolling the lawn, and they all went into the grocer's to help him choose some sweets. Henry bought the tea and put it for safety into his pocket, then they chose some boiled sweets of a particularly cheap and colourful brand. They next held a spirited exchange of grimaces with the grocer's boy, which degenerated into a scuffle and brought down a pyramid of tins of boot blacking. The grocer chased them out of the shop, and they emerged into the road feeling cheered and exhilarated.

It was Ginger's turn to push the pram, and he seized it with a new vigour.

"She'll yell if she wakes," Henry warned him, so Ginger abated his vigour somewhat.

"Look here," said William, "I've not thought of anything exciting to do at Ethel's party to-morrow yet. Let's all try an' think of somethin'."

"Let's all dress up as robbers an' dash in at them," suggested Ginger.

"Let's set some mice loose among them," said Henry, "I can get some mice."

"Let's put a grass snake on the tea-table," said Douglas. "That'd scare 'em stiff."

"But I want something they'd *enjoy*," said William.

"Well, they'd enjoy all those things," said Ginger, "they'd enjoy talking about them an' tellin' other people about them afterwards, even if they didn't enjoy them at the time. It'd be somethin' to make them *remember* the party by; if a party's ordinary and dull, there's nothin' to make people remember it by."

"An' I'll tell you another thing," said Douglas, "And that's letting a bit of gunpowder off while they're having tea. That's *great* fun for them. And another is putting glue on the hats, so that when they go home they can't get their hats off. I bet they'd laugh like anything at that——"

They had reached Henry's house now, and Henry, stopping short, began to gaze with startled interest at the sleeping baby.

"I say!" he cried excitedly.

He craned further into the pram. When he withdrew his face was pale with horror.

"I say," he said, "that's not ours."

"Not your what?" said William.

"Not our baby," said Henry.

"*Course* it is," said William; "what makes you think it isn't?"

"Ours doesn't look like that."

"There isn't any difference in babies," said William, "they all look just the same. You can't *possibly* tell any diff'rence."

"I can," protested Henry vehemently. "When you know them *very* well there is a difference, and I tell you, this one isn't ours."

"Well, I bet your mother won't know," said William. "I bet *she* won't see any difference. It looks just the same to me, an' I bet it looks just the same to anyone."

"I tell you it *doesn't*," said Henry, "and its clothes are different. She'll see its clothes are different anyway."

William realised the force of this argument.

"Couldn't we say we'd bought it some new clothes for a present?" he suggested, not very convincingly.

"No," said Henry rather irritably. "She'd know we couldn't have. An' I keep tellin' you she knows its face."

"Well, I believe it's the same one," said William. "You've just got muddled, that's all it is. You're trying to swank, pretending that you can tell a difference in babies when everyone knows there isn't any. How *could* it be a different one anyway? We just took it to the shop and brought it back. How could it have got changed?"

"It isn't our pram either," said Henry, who was closely examining the equipage, "it's quite different."

"There *was* another pram outside the shop," said

Ginger, thoughtfully, "p'raps I took the wrong one."

"I'll run back and see if ours is there," said Henry.

He ran off down the road and soon reappeared, paler than ever.

"There isn't any pram at all there now," he said. "I've been right in the shop and there's *nothing*." He glanced with distaste at the infant who still slept peacefully in the pram. "Well, I can't take *that* one home. She'd kick up an *awful* row."

"Look here," said William, "I expect someone took yours by mistake. I expect it's always happening. Well, they *do* all look just the same whatever you say—so of *course* it's always happening. I expect no one ever ends up a single day with the same baby they started out with . . . an' I don't see what you're making all this fuss about. It's a *baby*, isn't it? Well, what more d'you want? What does it matter if it's not the same as the other? Someone else has got the other, so *they're* all right, an' *you're* all right. Oh, very well . . . if you say your mother'd make a fuss . . . . Well, I'll go round the village an' try'n' find yours."

"An' I'll go round the other way," said Ginger.

They set off with a purposeful air in opposite directions.

Henry and Douglas were left with the pram and the sleeping stranger. Henry kept throwing uneasy glances through the hedge.

"I say," he said, "I'm scared stiff she'll come out after the tea and see it's the wrong one. She'll go *mad*. You don't know what they're like about babies. Put it here where the hedge is nice and thick an' I'll go in and give her the tea and tell her that we're taking the baby out for a bit of a walk. She'll be jolly glad because she's busy, and it's generally out till tea-time."

Cautiously he entered the gate. Soon the voice of his mother was wafted through the hedge to the waiting Douglas.

"How *could* you be so careless, Henry! I simply daren't *think* of what might have happened. . . . Just going off like that and forgetting all about her! I shall never, never, *never* trust you with her again. Yes, Mrs. Hanshaw brought her back a minute ago. Found her outside the grocer's shop. Fortunately she's still asleep. You simply aren't fit to be trusted with *anything*."

HENRY LOOKED FROM ONE PRAM TO THE OTHER, A NIGHTMARISH GRIN ON HIS FACE. "WHICH IS YOURS?" SAID WILLIAM.

Henry rejoined Douglas in the road, and they stood gazing at each other in helpless dismay. At that moment there reappeared the figure of William jauntily wheeling another pram.

"I say," he called exultantly, "I bet this is it. I found it outside another shop."

At the same moment there appeared from the other direction the figure of Ginger. He, too, was wheeling a pram. He did not at first see William. He called out:

"It's all right. I've got it. I found it outside a house."

Henry looked from one to the other, a nightmarish grin on his face.

"Which is yours?" said William. "I bet mine is."

"I bet *mine* is," put in Ginger.

"Neither is," said Henry, "we've got ours. Someone brought it back."

"I BET *MINE* IS HIS," PUT IN GINGER.

They gazed at the three prams with their sleeping cargoes, and the situation in all its horror gradually dawned upon them.

"Gosh!" said William. "*Three!*"

"We'd better take 'em back," said Ginger faintly.

"My mother was *mad* about ours," said Henry.

There came to William and Ginger a vision of three raging mothers.

"We can't take 'em back," said William apprehensively. "I vote—I vote we take them to the police station and say that we found someone kidnapping 'em and rescued 'em."

"They won't believe us," said Ginger sadly.

William on reflection agreed that probably they wouldn't.

"What are we going to *do* then?" demanded Douglas.

At that moment the voice of Henry's mother was heard urgently calling him.

"I'd better go," said Henry; "she'll only be coming out after me if I don't, and then she'll find all these others and kick up another row."

They agreed, and, with something of relief at his heart, Henry left the pram-infested scene. Douglas, Ginger, and William were left each with his attendant infant. They looked at each other helplessly.

"I vote we just leave them here an' creep away," said Ginger.

"We can't leave them outside Henry's house," said William. "It'd only get him into another row. Let's take them down the road a bit and leave them there."

Despondently they began to wheel their prams down the road.

"I bet wherever we leave them we'll get into a row," said William gloomily. "Someone'll be sure to see us with them. Seems 'str'ordin'ry to me that some people seem to have nothin' else to do but watch other people doin' things an' then tell about them afterwards to get 'em into rows."

At that moment a boy came alongside of them pushing a pram in a detached and hasty manner.

"Hello," he said, "you got to take *yours* to the baby show, too?"

William made a non-committal sound.

"Well, I think it's the limit, don't you?" said the boy. "I said why should I take it, and she said that she'd entered it and so it had to go, but she'd got a bad headache an' couldn't take it, and that I ought to be *proud* to take my little brother to a baby show an' a lot of stuff like that. Said it was sure to get a prize. Yes, it'll get a prize for yelling all right if it starts. Well, I don't want to be longer than I can help making a fool of myself pushing a beastly pram so I'll get on."

He continued his hurried and detached progress. He walked quickly and airily by the side of the pram, keeping two fingers only upon the handle to steer it and determinedly looking in the opposite direction, as if hoping to convince those he met that he had no connection whatever with the equipage and that it merely happened to be going of its own volition in the same direction. Somewhat cheered by this spectacle, William, Ginger, and Douglas began to follow after him in a row, each pushing his pram.

"A baby show," said William, "that'll be fine. We can just put them with the other prams an' leave them there. You see with a lot of prams, no one 'll notice three extra ones. We can just put 'em there an' creep away."

The boy in front with a deft and practised movement of his wrist had turned his pram into the gateway of a large garden. There on the lawn was a serried row of prams. The Outlaws put theirs at the end as unobtrusively as possible. No one seemed to have noticed their arrival. Several groups of women were standing about on the lawn talking.

"Now let's go," whispered William. "We'd better not all go at once or they'll see. We'll go one by one. . . . You go now, Ginger."

Ginger crept away in his best Red Indian style.

No one noticed his departure.

"Now you, Douglas," hissed William.

Douglas crept away with equal success. William watched his figure as it slunk through the bushes and then out through the gateway. He leant negligently on his pram handles waiting till Douglas should be quite out of sight. Then, just as he had decided to follow, he heard himself addressed in a sharp, imperious voice.

"Are you in charge of these prams?" An elegant woman in a long, black satin cloak and be-plumed hat stood in front of him, pointing a pair of lorgnettes at him.

The proprietary attitude in which William was leaning over his pram handles made the charge a difficult one to deny.

"Er—yes," he said guardedly, "I mean, I'm sort of in charge of them."

"Why aren't there any numbers on them then?"

"I don't know," said William.

The woman turned to another harassed-looking woman behind her.

"The whole thing's been most disgracefully mismanaged. Here are three more prams without numbers. I said particularly: 'Send the numbers round to the mothers beforehand so as to save time.' Were no numbers sent?" she said to William.

"No," said William.

A third woman came up and meekly affixed numbers to the prams.

The first woman was looking at William rather doubtfully.

"Did you say you were in charge of all three prams?" she said.

"Yes," replied William.

"I suppose one of them is your little brother?" she went on.

"They all are," said William, who thought that, cornered as he was, he might as well accept the situation in its entirety. It was never William's way to go in for half measures.

The lady looked at them still more doubtfully.

"Triplets?" she said.

William again made his non-committal noise. The lady evidently took it to mean assent.

"How curious to have them in three separate prams! You couldn't have brought them *all* surely?"

"Yes, I did," said William. "I push one pram for a bit along the road and then I fetch the second up to it, and then I fetch the third. And then I start again on the first."

"How very strange!" said the woman. "I should have thought it would be simpler to put them all in one large pram. They're quite small children. Why didn't your mother come with them?"

"She's ill," said William.

"I'm so sorry. I'm sure you're a great help to her with your three little brothers, aren't you?"

"Oh yes," said William, now firmly established in his own mind as brother to the three sleeping infants.

"Well, do suggest to her that she puts them all in one

large pram. It wouldn't be a bit overcrowded. And really taking out three prams in the way you describe seems an unnecessary labour—till they've got *much* older than this, anyway. Have you brought the form?"

"The form?" said William.

"Yes. Surely a form was sent to your mother for her to fill in?"

"No, it wasn't," said William.

"*There!*" said the woman again. "Another muddle. The thing's been *completely* mismanaged. Give me a form, please." The meek woman handed her a form. "And I ought to have been told that there would be triplets. They're a class by themselves, of course. I'll fill in the form now. Just answer the questions," she said to William, "and I'll fill in the answers. What illnesses have they had?"

"Lumbago," said William, remembering the complaint that had kept his father in bed for a day last week.

"*What?*"

"No, not lumbago," said William hastily. "I mean only one of them had lumbago just a bit. No, the illness that the other two had is——" he paused a moment. What was that thing that had kept Colonel Fortescue in bed all last holidays and so left the Outlaws in unofficial possession of his paddock? "Oh, I know, gout."

"Rubbish," said the woman indignantly. "Children of that age couldn't have gout."

"The doctor said he'd never known one have it before," argued William.

At the mention of the doctor the woman became less sure of her ground.

"Well, all I can say is *I've* never heard of it," she said and passed on hastily to the next question. "What have they been brought up on?"

"Brought up on?" said William.

"Yes, what do they eat?"

"Oh," said William, comprehending; "well, for breakfast they have sausages."

"*Sausages!*" said the lady horrified.

William realised that sausages was wrong.

"Only one of them has sausages," he said reassuringly, "the others have chops."

"*Chops!*"

Evidently chops was wrong, too.

"I only meant one of the other two has chops," said William hastily, "this one has kippers."

"*Kippers!*"

Evidently kippers was wrong, too. But at that moment one of the triplets awoke with a yell, and at once the other two, roused from sleep, joined in the chorus. Also at that minute William, turning sharply, saw three angry-looking women entering the gate. They were obviously mothers on the track of their missing young. Without a second's hesitation William dived into the bushes, plunged through the hedge, scrambled out into the road, and ran as fast as he could in the direction of his home. He had no doubt at all that the mothers would discover who he was and where he lived and all about him, but it would take a little time.

"Mother," he said breathlessly, entering the drawing-room, "I'll go and stay with Aunt Jane if I can go at once."

"Whatever's made you change your mind, dear?"

William tried to compose his features into their expression of shining virtue.

"Because you said you'd like me to go, and I want to please you."

Mrs. Brown looked slightly bewildered.

"MOTHER," SAID WILLIAM BREATHLESSLY, "I'LL GO AND STAY
WITH AUNT JANE IF I CAN GO AT ONCE."

"WHATEVER'S MADE YOU CHANGE YOUR MIND, DEAR?"

"Well, dear, I'll write to her to-night, and you can go
to her to-morrow."

"No," said William, "I want to go there now at once,
this minute. It won't be any use to-morrow."

Mrs. Brown looked still more bewildered.

"But why, dear?" she said.

"Because," said William unctuously, "I may not feel
like this to-morrow. I just feel now that I want to please
you and do what you want me to do, but I don't know
how long a feeling like that's going to last. It doesn't last

very long generally. I'm beginning to feel it going already. If I don't get off to Aunt Jane's now this minute, it'll have gone."

Mrs. Brown's thoughts went to Ethel. Ethel would find it very difficult to forgive her if she let slip this chance, appearing so miraculously and at the last minute, of a Williamless tennis party. . . .

"Very well, dear," she said, "I'll go and pack your things this minute. We'll send the wire from the station."

William was standing by the window, keeping an anxious eye on the point in the road where the three angry mothers would appear.

"Do be quick," he said, "I can feel that feeling going already. . . ."

In an incredibly short space of time Mrs. Brown was downstairs with his bag.

"Come along, dear," she said, "you needn't bother to change. We can just get the 'bus into Hadley and catch the four o'clock train."

They hurried to the end of the road and just caught the 'bus. As they sat there waiting for it to start, three angry-looking women wheeling prams were seen to turn into the lane that led to William's home. Mrs. Brown watched them with interest.

"I wonder where they're going," she said, then, "why, they're going to our house. How funny. . . . Yes, they're going up to our front door. I wonder what they want."

But William was gazing dreamily in front of him as if he did not hear her, and at that moment the 'bus started.

They just had time to wire to William's aunt before catching the train. William waved to his mother till the train took him out of her sight, then sank back into his corner of the carriage with a sigh of relief. His mother would be on her way home where the three angry women awaited her. . . . They couldn't do anything to him now of course, and they'd probably have forgotten all about it by the time he came home. It was a pity about Ethel's party. It would just have to be the dull sort of affair it usually was. Aunt Jane's . . . she was jolly dull, of course, but still he might manage to have quite a decent time. There was a pond in her garden, in which he could be shipwrecked from a raft, and a rockery that might be made to represent an impregnable mountain lair. There was a fat Pekinese in the opposite house into whose ordered life considerable excitement might be introduced.

William began to look forward with feelings of pleasurable anticipation to his visit to Aunt Jane.

Chapter 4

William and the Eastern Curse

William had not, however, really expected to enjoy his visit to Aunt Jane's, and on arriving he found things exactly as he had known they would be. The house was depressingly clean and tidy. Everything in it had its own place and was not to be moved or touched. Even the Pekinese in the opposite house had, it turned out, died of overeating the month before. Aunt Jane was tall and prim and what she called "house proud". She winced at the passage of William's boots over her parquet floors even when he did not attempt to slide on them. She met all his suggestions for the employment of his time with an unfailing: "No, William, *certainly* not." She did not want him to play in her garden, because he spoilt the flower-beds ("It isn't as if you kept to the grass, dear, and even the grass, with those heavy shoes——"). She did not want him to play out of her garden, because he always came home so dirty and untidy. She did not want him to play in the house, because he made a noise. She found a friend for him, a nice quiet boy whose interests centred entirely in the study of geography and the making of maps. After one meeting William announced to his aunt that he would not go out with that boy again, not if he was to be put to death by torture for it.

"I thought you'd find him so *interesting*, dear," she said wistfully. "I thought he'd do you *good*."

"Well, he hasn't done," said William firmly.

His aunt looked at him in pathetic bewilderment.

"I simply can't understand you, dear," she said. "I've always thought him such a *nice* boy."

She had plenty of suggestions in answer to William's demands as to what there was for him to do.

"Well, dear, there's a lot for you to do. You can sit quietly in the morning-room and read. I've got a complete set of the *Encyclopædia Britannica*, and I'm sure you'd find it interesting. One sees quite young children reading it in the advertisements. And, when you're tired of reading, you could go for a nice walk. There's a very interesting church in the village. Part of it Early Perpendicular. I'm sure you'd find that *most* interesting. You could spend a few hours looking round it, and then you could come home and read the article on Architecture in the *Encyclopædia Britannica*. Then in the afternoon you could go out with a notebook and make notes of all the wild flowers you see—keeping to the roads, of course, because the grass is always apt to be damp—and then you could spend the evening reading the article on Botany in the *Encyclopædia Britannica*. And you could make a little collection of pressed wild flowers. I think that you would find the time pass very quickly and happily in that way."

William surveyed this programme morosely, and finally consented to set off on what his aunt called a "botanical stroll", armed with a small tin in which to put his specimens.

He returned (late for lunch) covered with mud, and with his suit torn in several places. The only wild flowers that he had to show for his "walk" were a daisy and a dandelion, which, suddenly remembering the mission on which he was supposed to have gone, he had gathered in haste from the roadside just outside his aunt's gate. He had lost the tin. He explained that this was not his fault. He had been using it to dam a stream, and a farmer had come and chased him away before he could recover it. It was a farmer, too, he explained, who was solely responsible for his torn suit.

"I can get through a barbed-wire fence without tearing anything," said William. "I often have done. If he'd not been running after me and shouting at me, I'd 've got through it all right."

Aunt Jane raised her hand to her head with the expression of one who suffers acute mental anguish.

"But I said keep to the *road*, William," she said.

"Yes," said William unabashed, "I remember now that you said that. But I forgot it this morning. I've got a very poor memory."

Aunt Jane made him change into his best suit and sent his torn one into the kitchen for Molly, the maid, to mend. Aunt Jane also decreed that William must not set foot out of the house in his best suit, and, to make sure of this, sat with him in the drawing room reading the *Encyclopædia Britannica* article on Architecture to him aloud.

Neither Aunt Jane's mind nor William's was really concentrated upon the *Encyclopædia Britannica* article on Architecture. Both, in fact, contained one single thought, and the single thought was that it was high time that this visit of William's came to an end. Both of them, however, felt a certain delicacy about suggesting it.

Aunt Jane's eyelids began to droop. In the excitement of William's late return she had missed her afternoon nap.

AUNT JANE RAISED HER HAND TO HER HEAD WITH THE EXPRESSION
OF ONE WHO SUFFERS ACUTE MENTAL ANGUISH. "I SAID KEEP TO
THE *ROAD*, WILLIAM," SHE SAID.

"I'm just going up to my bedroom to write a few
letters, my boy," she said to William. "You might go
into the kitchen and see if Molly has finished mending
your other suit."

So William went into the kitchen where Molly, a
pretty, rosy-cheeked girl, sat by the window drawing
together the edges of one of William's famous three-

cornered tears. She greeted him with a friendly wink.

"Well, you young monkey," she said, "I bet the old girl's read you a proper lecture."

William had not given any attention to Molly till now, but suddenly he realised her as a person worth cultivating. The smile, the grin, the wink, and the friendly greeting, warmed his heart. They belonged to a world in which the *Encyclopædia Britannica* did not exist.

"It's the devil an' all to mend," she went on, half admiringly; "me own brother never made such a one, an' he was as big a scamp as you every bit. Anyway, come and sit down and tell me all about yourself while I finish it off."

So William sat down and told her all about himself, and when he had finished she told him all about herself. She was, it appeared, wooed by two suitors, and she did not know which to choose. One was the chauffeur-coachman next door, and the other was the baker's man. William, who knew them both, was deeply interested in the problem.

"James looks a treat in his uniform," said Molly, "an' he's smarter an' he's better off. But there—I always had a soft corner for George. I've tossed up over an' over again, but it always comes different. I tell you, I don't know *what* to do. It fair keeps me awake at nights."

"I like George best," said William.

She sighed.

"I dare say you do, but a boy's nothing to go by. I mean, the one you like best mightn't make me the best husband."

"I don't think James would make a good husband," said William.

She sighed again.

"That's just because George can blow smoke-rings and yodel," she said. "Boys always like him. But smoke-rings and yodelling isn't much good to a wife."

William knew both James and George more thoroughly than Molly realised. He was, in fact, deeply involved in hostilities with James. He had greeted both James and George with a challenging grimace on his first meeting. George had replied by a grimace that was unquestionably superior and had asked him if he would like a ride round the village in his baker's cart. During the ride he had yodelled for him and blown smoke-rings and at the end had let him help unharness Daisy, the horse. In William's eyes George was a demi-god. His relations with James were different. James, who was out with the car when they first met, had replied to his grimace by deliberately driving through a puddle so as to drench William in muddy water, and the next morning when out with the trap had given him a stinging flick of the whip. Thenceforward, whenever James met William in his capacity of chauffeur, he drove his car so near him as to precipitate him into the ditch, and, whenever he met him in his capacity of coachman, he flicked him neatly but painfully with his whip. James was one of those men who believe that small boys exist to be teased. But William possessed a grown-up sister, and he knew that women are incalculable in their attitude to admirers of the opposite sex. With Ethel, the fact that William disliked a particular suitor generally predisposed Ethel in that particular suitor's favour. So he said little to Molly about the rival merits of James and George, confining himself to discussing with her ways and means of choosing between them. The ways they tried were numerous and intriguing. They threw apple peel over their shoulders to see what initial it formed. It formed unmistakably the letter S, but, as Molly knew no one whose name began with that letter, the experiment carried them no further. They made spills of the same length, one with the name James written upon it and the other George, lit them at the same second, and watched to see which should burn the longer. They burnt out at the identical second. They wrote their names on paper, put them in a hat, shook them up, and let Molly draw one out. She drew four times. Twice she drew James and twice George. She wrote their names yet again on small pieces of paper and put them beneath her pillow to see which she would dream of. She dreamed of the pig that had shared her home in her childhood. It was a handsome, friendly pig, but did not even remotely suggest either George or James.

William, in a conscientious desire to help her, cultivated the acquaintance of her suitors yet further. He went to the next door garage, and in all good faith offered to help James clean the car. James playfully directed the full stream of the hose upon him. After that William confined his attention to George, who let him harness and unharness Daisy and spent many patient hours trying to teach him to yodel.

Aunt Jane was engaged in preparing an address on "The New Thought" for the "New Era Society", of which she was vice-president, and she was glad that William should spend his time quietly anywhere and with anyone as long as he did not disturb her. She found his yodel-practising inexpressibly painful, but tried to combat it with the exercise of the New Thought. As she sat at her little desk, trying to write her address, while William, going to bed above her, filled the house with horrible and raucous strains that changed with nerve-shattering suddenness from bass to tenor, she addressed her mind over and over again with the words: "You are poised and in harmony. No outside disharmony can disturb you."

Her mind, however, had quite different ideas on the subject, and persisted in being disturbed by the outside disharmony of William's yodelling. William, when remonstrated with, was profusely apologetic.

"I'm sorry," he would say, "I thought I was doing it low so as you wouldn't hear. I keep forgettin' that you don't like music."

William, in his self-appointed capacity of umpire, liked to be present at the frequent conversations that Molly held with her suitors at the kitchen gate. Though he was an unqualified supporter of George, he had to admit that James was the better conversationalist. Moreover, James always had the local news and gossip at his finger-ends.

"Old Marlow's dead," he said solemnly one evening leaning over the kitchen gate. "Ill-wished that man was."

"Ill-wished!" jeered Molly; "you don't believe in them things surely!"

But it appeared that James did believe in them things.

"Why, I've known of cases—well, you'd hardly believe them," he ended feebly.

"You tell me an' see if I'll believe them," challenged Molly.

"Well, of course," he admitted, "things like that aren't so common in England. It's in the East they happen most. I knew a man once that had lived in the East, and the things he told me——"

The silence was made eloquent by James's solemnly rounded eyes.

"Go on," said Molly still incredulous, "tell us some

of the things he told you."

James, seeing William standing within reach, seized his arm and twisted it half mechanically, then relapsed into solemnity.

"Well," he said, "it's true. This man who told me vouched for its truth. I can tell you I think twice before I ever annoy anyone from the East. They can put curses on you."

Molly was impressed despite herself.

"What sort of curses?" she said. "Go on! Tell us a bit more."

"They can put a curse of animals or insects onto people," said James slowly. "Well, honestly, you'd hardly believe it. They can put—say—a cat curse onto you, so that wherever you go there's cats. Cats everywhere, and you can't get rid of them, because, if you harm them in any way, it's you that's hurt, just as if someone had made you in wax and stuck pins in. And they generally put in the curse that one of them—say, the tenth you see—is fatal. And it always is. This man told me of some awful curses like that. Snakes one man had, and the seventh snake bit him and killed him, though it wasn't a real snake at all. The man that put the curse on him had told him that the seventh snake would kill him, and it did."

Molly threw back her head and laughed.

"I never heard such nonsense," she said.

James stared at her gloomily.

"You wouldn't call it nonsense if you knew some of the things this man told me," he said.

"Go on!" laughed Molly, her dark eyes sparkling. "Can't you find anything more interesting to talk to a girl about?"

James moved nearer her, and, replying to the challenge

of her eyes, found something more interesting to talk to a girl about.

That evening Molly grew still more confidential to William.

"It's no good me goin' on like this an' not being able to make up my mind," she said. "I must give them a test same as people do in books."

"What sort of a test?" said William.

Molly wrinkled her brow.

"Well, that's what I've got to make up my mind about," she said. "The test the girl in the last book I read gave, was pretending that she'd lost all her money, then the one that wasn't really worthy of her chucked her, and the other one stuck to her. And he was rewarded, of course, because she hadn't really lost her money."

"Well, you do that," said William with interest. "Tell them you've lost your money."

"They know I've not got any money, so it wouldn't make any difference," said Molly. "But I've made up my mind to give them a test, and I'm going to think hard what test to give them."

"Yes, an' I'll think hard too," said William helpfully, "we'll both think hard all to-morrow, an' to-morrow night we'll decide."

The next evening he joined Molly in the kitchen as usual. Aunt Jane was now wrestling with an address on "The World of Nature". "The New Thought" had got so far beyond her that she had had to give it up in favour of something on which the *Encyclopædia Britannica* was more explicit.

"I've thought of a ripping test," said William excitedly. "Have the one that can make the best ducks and drakes on a pond. I bet anyone that can make good ducks and drakes must be nice."

George, William knew, was the best maker of ducks and drakes for miles around. But his deep plot for making George the winning candidate did not succeed. Molly shook her head.

"No," she said. "I've thought of something much better than that. It was in a book I was reading last night after you went to bed, and in it the man was out walking with the girl, and they came to a place that was under water, and the girl said that she wanted to go to the other side, and the man just picked her up and carried her across, and didn't care how wet he got. Well, I think it was beautiful, don't you?"

"No, I don't," said William, "I think it was silly. I bet I wouldn't do that. Not for anyone."

"Yes, but you aren't in love," said Molly. "I think it's beautiful, and that's what I'm going to do. I'm going to go out for a walk with the two of them together on Sunday afternoon, and I'm going to take them down to Forster's meadow where it's flooded, and I'm going to see which will carry me over."

"But you could go round by the path," objected William. "The path isn't flooded."

"Yes, but I'll say I don't want to go round by the path," said Molly firmly, "I'll say I want to go to Mereham over the meadow. And I'll see which will carry me over. . . ."

William considered the situation gloomily. There was something flamboyant and theatrical about James. He would quite probably offer to carry her across, even if he punished her for it afterwards. George, on the other hand, was simple, and endowed with a large fund of common sense. If she could get to Mereham as well by the path, George would naturally object to wading over his knees through a flood. George would be kind but firm. George would not see any point in making a fool of himself. George, in short, would fail in the "test".

"I think it's a rotten test," said William. "If I were you I'd make it yodelling. I think it would be jolly nice to have a husband who could yodel."

"No," said Molly firmly, "I've made up my mind, and that's the test I'm going to have. And you've got to *promise* not to tell either of them."

Reluctantly William promised. He felt gloomy and apprehensive. He wanted George to marry Molly. He was convinced that Molly was too good for James. And it would be James, he was certain, who would triumphantly pass the "test".

That evening he sat on the fence, dangling his feet and wondering how, short of breaking his promise to Molly, he could make George pass the "test". George let him help unharness his horse every evening. George coached him kindly and painstakingly in his not-yet-successful efforts at yodelling. George even gave him an occasional bun left over from his "round". While James——

Suddenly the next-door car, driven by James, came into sight. The road was narrow and deeply pitted, and the pits were filled with water from the recent rain. A man was walking along the road, his head buried deep on his chest, his hat pulled low over his eyes. James, grinning, performed his favourite trick, driving his car as near to the pedestrian as possible and splashing him from head to foot with water. Then he turned round, still grinning, to enjoy his victim's discomfiture. His victim had lifted his head angrily, revealing a black face and white, furiously rolling eyes. He shouted some words they could not hear, shook his fist, then turned and resumed his walk.

James's mouth had dropped open, his face had paled. He drew up, and, forgetting to twist William's arm or push him off his perch, said: "Did you hear what he said?"

"No," said William.

"He—he was an Eastern, wasn't he?"

"Oh, yes," said William, "he was an Eastern all right."

"Cripes!" said James aghast, "I wish I'd heard what he said."

"It sounded like a curse," said William, enjoying James's dismay.

James's face turned from white to yellow. His eyes bulged and his hands trembled so much that, continuing on his way, he nearly took the gate off its hinges as he re-entered his employer's home.

William's spirits brightened. James would live in terror of a curse for many days to come. William felt avenged for the ills he had received at the hands of James. Then his spirits clouded again. James would still pass the test triumphantly to-morrow.

Then he completely forgot everything about James and George and Molly. For down the road was coming a familiar figure . . . a small, pied dog with a head too big for its body and a strange and unexpected tail. It was William's mongrel, Jumble. It had found life at home dull without him and had followed him to Aunt Jane's. It was travel-stained from its long journey, but it greeted William with ecstatic and uproarious delight. William, as deeply touched at the reunion as Jumble, gathered him into his arms with affectionate congratulation.

"Well done, old chap. You're a jolly clever dog, aren't you, coming all this way. Good old Jumble! Good old boy! I bet you're hungry. Come along——"

Dismay settled on his face again. Aunt Jane disliked dogs.

She would not let Jumble stay there. She would insist on Jumble's being sent home at once.

Very cautiously, very slowly, William led Jumble to the little shed at the bottom of Aunt Jane's garden and tied him up. Then he went indoors to consult Molly. Molly was sympathetic. Molly, it appeared, had a weakness for mongrels. "I had one at home. No breed at all, it wasn't, but as faithful and loving as any dog ever made. An' the first thing I'm going to do when I'm married is to set up a dog."

Together they took food down to Jumble. Jumble won her heart at once by sitting up to beg despite his weariness. Together they watched him eat the meaty bones and the biscuits that they had brought down for him.

"She'll send him back," said Molly. "She'll send him back sure as Fate. She can't abear 'em, says they mess up the place. She'll tell the gardener to take him back by train to-morrow. Sure as Fate she will."

William was silent for a few seconds then gave a sudden gasp.

"*Tell* you what! I've got an idea. Let's keep him here. She won't know he's here. She never comes out here. I can sneak out with him sometimes through the hedge to take him for a walk. An' we can bring food to him down here. It's a *fine* idea."

Molly hesitated, and finally yielded. The prospect of an impending engagement to either James or George according to the results of the "test", made her feel independent and inclined to a gesture of defiance.

"Sure, my soul's my own," she said, "an' I've a right to give shelter to a fellow-creature if I like. An' if she finds it an' gives me notice she's welcome to. I'll be glad to shake the dust of her off my feet, the old fool.''

At this moment Aunt Jane called William indoors and gave him some letters to post. William, after due consideration, decided not to take Jumble. For one thing, Jumble was tired. For another, he did not wish to risk detection the first night of Jumble's stay. Instead he took a ball with which he was in process of perfecting a trick. The trick consisted in throwing it over his left shoulder from behind and catching it in front. William had only begun to practise it yesterday, and he was very much pleased with the progress he had made. He had already almost decided to be an acrobat when he grew up. As soon as Jumble was rested, he would start training Jumble for their joint career. He had gratifying visions of himself, clothed in tights, balancing Jumble (standing on one paw) on one hand, and with the other throwing a swift succession of balls over his left shoulder from behind and catching them again in front.

Just as he was passing the next door gate the ball slipped from his hand and flew over the gate, landing at the feet of James, who stood idly watching a garden fire. Grinning at William, James picked up the ball, held it tantalisingly aloft, then dropped it into the flames. William walked on, scowling angrily. Then he stopped suddenly as if struck by an idea. The scowl cleared from his face, and a beatific smile took its place.

*   *   *

James, spick and span, in his Sunday best, lounged elegantly at the back gate of Aunt Jane's house, completely ignoring George, who, less elegant though also in his Sunday best, lounged there also. They were both waiting for Molly. The arrangement was an unusual one.

Generally she went out with them on alternate Sundays, but this Sunday, though neither James nor George yet knew it, was the Sunday of the "test". After a few minutes Molly, flushed and pretty and demure, joined them.

"I thought you wouldn't mind us all three going out together," she said brightly. "I'd like to go over Mereham way if it's all the same to you."

Evidently it was all the same to them. The three set off towards Mereham. Molly's bright eyes sparkled. She enjoyed the situation to the full. She did most of the talking. George was generally rather silent. James, on the other hand, was generally a fluent talker, but to-day a constrained silence held him too. A close observer would have noticed that he was nervous. He threw quick, apprehensive glances about him as he walked. He was distinctly white about the gills. He kept one hand in his pocket, tightly clutching a note. It was an anonymous note, and he had received it last night. It began without any form of address:

"I have put the curse of dogs upon you. If you harm any of these dogs the harm will come back to you. The fifth dog will be fatal.

      The Eastern you splashed this afternoon."

James had tried to make light of this to himself, but he had passed an uneasy night. This morning he had not even tried to make light of it. For the curse had taken effect. He was a doomed man. As he walked by Molly, glancing nervously about him and fingering the fateful note, his mind went over the events of that morning. On going down to the garage he had heard a strange noise from the car. He had opened the door, and to his horror a dog had jumped out. He had remembered the contents of the note just in time to restrain himself from throwing anything after it as it ran off, but it had taken him a long time to recover from the shock sufficiently to rub up the brasswork of the car, as was his custom on Sunday mornings. He had then gone to the woodshed to chop some firewood for the cook—one of his daily duties. Immediately on his opening the door a dog shot out and past him. He then faced the horrible truth. He was a man under a dog curse. He took a much longer time than usual to chop the firewood, then went to the greenhouse to water the chrysanthemums—another of his Sunday duties, as the gardener did not come on that day. This time the dog almost knocked him down in its frantic exit. He watched its vanishing figure with bulging eyes, and then took out a handkerchief to mop his brow. That was the third dog (all exactly alike—they were alike in these curses of course). The fifth was the fatal one.

Feeling shaken, he decided to go to his room over the garage and rest. He opened his door with the glad feeling of one who goes to a familiar refuge where danger cannot penetrate, but the feeling was short-lived. A dog—exactly like the other three dogs—shot out, tumbled head over heels down the stairs and vanished from sight. And so it was that James walked with less than his accustomed swagger, and glanced furtively from side to side. Molly, taking his silence for the embarrassment of one who suffers the pangs of love, was not displeased by it. She chattered gaily to both of her suitors impartially. The road turned a sharp corner, and there in front of them lay the flooded meadows. The trio stopped, and Molly looked from one to the other beneath demurely lowered lashes.

"I want to get across," she murmured. "What shall I do?"

"I WANT TO GET ACROSS," MOLLY MURMURED. "WHAT SHALL I
DO?"

"The other path isn't under water," said George
reasonably, "we can go round by that."

"I don't want to go by the other path," said Molly, "I
want to go by the path through the meadows."

There was a silence.

"Can't—can't either of you think of a way?" said
Molly, smiling bewitchingly at James.

But James did not return the smile. His face was grey, and he was staring with a gaze of petrified horror at the fifth dog, that sat just beyond the strip of water. William lay at ease in the shadow of the hedge. Jumble sat in the sunlight, watching the water with friendly and enquiring interest. William had had a tiring day. First of all he had had to elicit from Molly a detailed account of James's Sunday activities. He had done it very cunningly, pretending that he was thinking of becoming a chauffeur himself when he grew up. The rest of the business had been much more difficult, requiring on William's part the utmost finesse and dexterity. To glide unseen under cover of the bushes with Jumble in his arms, to slip Jumble into James's next objective, retrieve him still unseen on his escape, and put him ready to be re-discovered, had needed all William's resource. Fortunately Jumble and William had often played Red Indians together, and therefore the whole proceeding was less startling to Jumble than it might otherwise have been. The only part of it he really objected to was being shut up in strange places without William, but Jumble was a sensible dog and knew that it was all part of the game, and that in that particular game he wasn't supposed to bark. He had unlimited faith in William, and was convinced that it would all come right in the end. It had been a brilliant inspiration of William's to make the fourth appearance of Jumble take place in James's own bedroom. He had guessed that by that time James would want to go somewhere to think the situation over quietly.

Suddenly Jumble noticed that one of the three people on the other side of the water was the Girl, the nice Girl, the Girl who had welcomed and fed him last night. He gave a shrill bark of excited recognition, and, plunging into the water, began to swim in her direction. With a wild cry James turned and fled, fled with such alacrity that in a few seconds he had completely vanished from the landscape.

Molly looked after him with tears of discomfiture in her eyes. George's manly heart was stirred by her distress.

"What is it, honey?" he said.

"I thought—I thought one of you would carry me over," said Molly forlornly.

Without a word George picked her up and carried her across to the waiting William.

*   *   *

William went into the drawing-room where his aunt was talking to the lady next door, and sat down patiently to wait till her visit should be over. He hoped that the sight of him would bring her visit to a premature conclusion. He had often noticed with secret gratification that his entry cleared his mother's drawing-room of guests.

"*So* annoying," William's aunt was saying, "I don't mean that she isn't far from perfect. In some ways she's *hopeless*. But I'd taken a lot of trouble training her, and *just* when I've begun to get her into my ways she tells me she's going to marry the baker's man next month. *Most* tiresome!"

"They're *all* tiresome," said the lady next door. Her tone showed more concern for her own troubles than for Aunt Jane's. "There's James now. I've always found him *most* satisfactory, and all of a sudden he turns peculiar."

"How 'peculiar'?" said William's aunt with perfunctory interest. She thought that Mrs. Bellews might have shown a little more sympathy about Molly.

"Well, I get a complaint from Mr. Jones at The Hawthorns that when he was coming home from the rehearsal at the Village Hall—he and some others are doing a sort of minstrel show with blacked faces in aid of the Organ Fund. I'm surprised at the Vicar for allowing it. I shan't go. I always find that sort of minstrel show vulgar. Anyway, he says that when he was coming back from the rehearsal James passed him in the car and deliberately drove into a puddle to splash him. It's *quite* ridiculous, of course. James is always *most* careful. It must have been some other chauffeur. He couldn't *possibly* recognise anyone with his face covered with that revolting black stuff anyway. But I sent for James and questioned him just as a matter of form, and he behaved most peculiarly."

"In what way?" said Aunt Jane, interested despite herself.

"Stared at me in the wildest fashion, his mouth wide open and his eyes nearly starting out of his head. And gave a *dreadful* sort of laugh. I told him to go and lie down till he felt better. It may be just the heat or, of course, it may be the beginning of insanity. I once had a housemaid——"

She caught William's eye fixed upon her with a stony glare, and decided to put off the story of the housemaid till another time. One never knew how much children understood nor what they would repeat. She rose and took her leave, patting William vaguely upon the head and thinking what a very unattractive-looking child he was.

As soon as she had gone William turned to his aunt and said abruptly: "My dog's come."

"Your what, dear?" said Aunt Jane bewildered.

"My dog's come," repeated William impatiently, "an' I 'spect you don't want him here."

"*Certainly* not, dear," said Aunt Jane firmly, "the animal must be sent home at once."

"Well, you see," said William slowly, "it wouldn't go back with anyone but me. It would bite anyone but me, so that they'd prob'ly get hydrophobia. So I'd better take him back. An'" (he fixed her with an unblinking eye), "it's not worth while me coming back here to finish up my visit once I've gone home, is it? I'd better stay there, hadn't I?"

Aunt Jane brightened visibly. She badly wanted a few quiet days with her address. She'd given up "The World of Nature" as being too crude and had begun to write an address on "The Duty of Happiness". But she wanted quiet for concentration, and it was curious how disturbing William's presence was, even when he was comparatively silent.

"Yes, dear," she said, "I shall be sorry to lose you, but I think it's an *excellent* idea."

Chapter 5

The New Neighbour

The house next door had been unoccupied for so long that William had begun to look upon its garden as his own property. Not that he found it at all exciting or took any real interest in it. It was too near his home for that. He could not trespass in it without being exposed to the full view of any of his family who chose to look out of the window, and he could not take his friends to play in it without one of his family's poking a head over the fence to tell him to come out at once and stop making that deafening noise. Still, there it was—part of his territory, a neglected, tumbling-to-pieces, three storey house, and a garden that was a waste expanse of old tins, broken pots, and the heterogeneous collection of rubbish that marked a long period of To-Let-ness. William thought of it as his castle and stronghold and, even though he seldom entered it, liked to imagine it peopled with picturesquely attired brigands awaiting orders from him before they set off on their day's work. He would often lean out of his window as he was dressing and give his orders to an imaginary brigand wearing sash, peaked cap, and innumerable cutlasses, who was leaning out of the corresponding window of the empty house.

"Go down to the railway this morning, an' hold up the London express, an' get all the money on it, an' this afternoon go to Ringers Hill, an' take anyone prisoner who comes there, an' hold 'em up to ransom.''

It gave him great satisfaction to commend his own particular enemies to the care of his brigand followers.

"Go and capture Mr. Jones an' keep him 'prisoned for a week, an' give him only dry bread to eat, an' p'raps that'll teach him to keep me in on half-holidays doin' beastly sums.''

William gathered from the conversation of grown-ups that there was very little likelihood of a new tenant's coming to the house. It was inconvenient and behind the times. It had no electric light. It had not even electric bells, only the old-fashioned wired bells with handles that you pulled.

"*Nobody*," William had heard people say again and again, "would *ever* take the house as it is.''

It was, therefore, with a sense of personal aggrievement that William heard that the house had been let, and that the tenant was going to move into it immediately. He called together his brigands, told them the news, and ordered them to evacuate the stronghold and take up their position on Ringers Hill, where he would send his further orders. He felt strangely desolate and at the mercy of his enemies when they departed, marching in step, a band in front of them, their cutlasses gleaming in the sun.

His spirits did not rise on sight of the new occupant of the house, a tall, powerfully made man with a face suggestive of a gorilla suffering from acute indigestion. He stood in the front garden as the furniture vans were unpacked, uttering ferocious bellows that were evidently intended to be directions, and threatening with his stick anyone who got in his way.

He then went round to the back garden. William, who had been an interested spectator in the front, also went round to the back and was just preparing to climb onto the fence in order to see all that was to be seen, when he was caught and overwhelmed by an avalanche of pots and pans and tins and old iron and rubbish of all sorts that came hurtling over the fence. The new tenant was getting rid of the extraneous matter that cumbered his ground by the simplest means to hand. Doubtless he took for granted that the rubbish had been thrown there by his next door neighbour, and so, like curses and chickens, might go home to roost. In ordinary circumstances William would have been rather amused than otherwise at seeing the garden, over which he considered that his father made himself so unnecessarily disagreeable, thus desecrated, and would have looked forward with feelings of pleasurable anticipation to watching his father's reactions to the sight. But circumstances were not quite ordinary. His father had gone abroad on business and was not here to defend himself. He had spent the entire afternoon and evening before his departure tidying the garden, and William, who when his father was at home felt only annoyance at the zeal that so circumscribed his own activities in the garden, felt now a sudden fury at seeing the trim lawn and immaculate flower-beds littered with tin cans, broken pots and innumerable pieces of old iron.

Without a moment's hesitation he began to gather them up and fling them back. They were immediately returned. He flung them back again. A fierce battle followed. William's forehead was cut by a tin can, but on flinging a broken pail over, he had the satisfaction of hearing a bellow of pain and the opening and shutting of a door as if his enemy had retreated. He flung the other things over without their being returned. The next day the neighbour wore a bandage round his head, and a dust cart arrived in the afternoon to take away the rubbish.

William felt exhilarated and quite willing to enter upon friendly relationship with his fallen foe.

The following afternoon he and Ginger were playing a game of tennis on a simplified system invented by William, when a ball went over the fence into their new neighbour's garden.

William and Ginger discussed the situation. Ginger was for climbing the fence, getting the ball, and making a dash for safety. William, however, was for behaving handsomely and giving the neighbour an opportunity of doing the same.

"No, I'll go round an' say I'm sorry I let it go over and may I get it. P'raps he's quite decent really. P'raps he thought we wouldn't mind that rubbish in our garden. Anyway, if he won't let us fetch it, we'll have to get over the fence, of course."

Boldly he walked up to the front door. A forbidding-looking maid opened it.

"Please," said William politely, "my ball's gone over the fence by accident. Please I'd be very much obliged if you'd kin'ly let me come over and get it."

The maid disappeared and returned in a few moments.

"He says you can come over the fence and get it."

"Thank you very much indeed," said William gratefully. "Please tell him thank you very much *indeed*."

He returned to his back garden and lightly swarmed the fence, surveying with interest the expanse of waste land and overgrown shrubs that had so lately been occupied by his brigands. The removal of the rubbish had made the whole place look larger than it had looked before. He saw his ball in the further corner of the garden and went across to get it. It was just as he was stooping to pick it up that he suddenly caught sight of the new occupant of the house, crouching behind a bush near the fence, armed with a stick. William's mind worked swiftly. The enemy's plan was, of course, to cut off his retreat. He picked up his ball as if he had seen nothing and sauntered slowly towards the bush in which the enemy lay concealed. Then, at the very second in which the enemy sprang out of his hiding-place, William, whose muscles were braced for this moment, dodged nimbly aside and vaulted over the fence. The stick struck the wood with terrific force just as William alighted in his own garden.

"*Well*," said William, "well, that settles it. I won't make peace with him now, not if he comes beggin' me on bended knees."

There seemed, however, to be no chance of his enemy's coming and begging him on bended knees for peace.

Mrs. Brown, quite unaware that William had already unofficially made the new neighbour's acquaintance, paid her formal call on him, and, finding her ring unanswered, put her cards through the letter-box.

"I *don't* like the look of him," she said, "but one must be neighbourly."

The new neighbour evidently did not share her views, for the cards, torn into small fragments, were returned to the Browns' letter-box, before the end of the day. William would not have thought anything of this, had not Robert, his nineteen-year-old brother, taken it as a deadly affront and one that in his father's absence it devolved upon him to avenge.

"I don't see that it's done anyone any harm," said William, who was of tougher material than to recognise such subtle forms of insult. "I mean, she can stick it together now and use it again if she wants to, and she couldn't have if he'd kept it. Well, I can't see what harm it does anyone."

"I dare say you can't," said Robert scathingly, "but it's the sort of thing that I'd have called him out for and fought a duel with him a hundred years ago."

"I don't see how you could have done," said William, "you weren't alive a hundred years ago."

"Oh, shut up," said Robert. "You don't know what you're talking about. If father were here, of course, it would be different. I mean, I shouldn't feel called upon to take the matter up. As it is, I shall go round to him and tell him what I think of him, and—well, I shall go round to him and tell him what I think of him."

"May I come with you?" said William, deeply interested in the situation.

"Of course you mayn't," said Robert, and added in a sinister voice: "If the man refuses to apologise I may have to use violence, and the fewer witnesses there are to it the better. In any case it's nothing whatever to do with you. I don't want you poking your nose into it. You've not come across the man in any way, so you can kindly keep out of it."

William forbore to describe exactly how he had come across the man, aware that if he did so Robert might consider him partly responsible for the state of affairs, and exact vengeance from him as well as from the man.

"Well," he said, adopting a mysterious tone of voice, and thinking of his band of brigands at present encamped on Ringers Hill, "if you want anything really *ruthless* done to him just you let me know."

"Oh, shut up," said Robert again.

Mrs. Brown, informed of his intention of going round

to wrest an apology from their neighbour, was placidly disapproving.

"I really *shouldn't*, dear. After all, what *does* it matter?"

But Robert was stern and haughty with the overwhelming sternness and hauteur of nineteen years.

"You don't understand, mother. A man can't pass over an insult of this sort to his womenfolk. In insulting you he's insulted all of us."

"But I'm so afraid, dear," said Mrs. Brown, "that you'll do something violent, and then, of course, there'll be trouble."

"I won't hurt the man," promised Robert darkly, "more than he deserves."

He put on his best suit for the visit, and took the torn-up fragments of the visiting-cards in his hand.

"I don't want to be inhuman," he said as he set off, "but I've a good mind to make him actually swallow them."

The front door of the next house could be seen from the corner of an attic window, and William lost no time in posting himself at this point of vantage.

He hoped that Robert would make the man actually swallow the pieces.

He watched his elder brother walk with purposeful step up the short drive to the front door. There he stopped and spent a few moments straightening his tie (already quite straight) before he pulled the old-fashioned bell.

William, from his post at the attic window, heard the bell jangle loudly in the kitchen region. After a few minutes the front door opened, and the gorilla-like figure appeared on the threshold.

Robert took a step backwards, then with an air of

desperate courage thrust out the hand containing the torn-up visiting-cards and said in a high-pitched voice: "What do you mean by this, sir?"

The fist of the new neighbour shot out, and Robert fell ignominiously down the short flight of steps from the front door, rolling for some distance along the drive. The figure of the new neighbour then vanished, and the front door was shut with a resounding bang. Robert picked himself up slowly and staggered down to the gate. William returned to the drawing-room, where his mother sat sewing.

"I do hope that Robert won't do anything violent," she said, drawing her needle out of her piece of work.

"I don't think he will," William reassured her.

"I wish I'd said that he wasn't to go," she went on. "It would be dreadful if that man brought an action for assault against him."

"I don't think that'll happen," said William again soothingly.

After a few minutes Robert came in. He had first gone upstairs to brush his suit. He looked rather pale.

"Oh, Robert," said his mother, "I do hope you didn't lose your temper."

"N-no," said Robert thoughtfully as if he weren't quite sure, "I don't think I actually lost my temper."

"What happened, dear?"

Robert struck the attitude of a strong, silent man. A sinister little smile played round his lips.

"I don't think you'll have any more trouble with him," he said.

After that Robert never referred to their new neighbour and always went the longer way to the village in order not to pass his house. William was left with the sense of a deadly family insult unavenged. For some time his imaginary army of bandits assuaged his uneasy spirit. Acting under his orders, they kidnapped the new neighbour a dozen times a day, they held him captive in lonely mountain strongholds, they forced him to do menial tasks for them, they tore up his visiting-cards and knocked him down flights of steps. They hung him from high pine trees and gallows and flung his body to the vultures. But this was all slightly unsatisfactory as long as the gorilla-like figure of the new neighbour could be seen quite unharmed going about as usual in the garden and village. The situation, however, soon got beyond the help of his bandits, for William a few mornings later met Miss Morall, an unoffensive maiden lady who lived on the other side of the gorilla, with traces of tears on her cheeks.

"Oh, William," she said unsteadily, "I was coming to warn you. My poor little Prince has gone."

"Gone?" repeated William.

"Poisoned, William. That dreadful man next door. I went round to him and he didn't attempt to deny it. He said he'd poison any other dog that he found in his garden . . . I thought I must warn you because of Jumble, William. . . . I'm simply heartbroken. It isn't as if a dog could do any harm in that wilderness. I'd go to law about it if I'd got any money. No, I don't suppose I would, because it wouldn't bring my Prince back. . . ."

William, horrified and indignant, murmured his sympathy and ran quickly homeward. He had known and liked Prince, a jolly little Yorkshire terrier. He thought of Jumble, his own beloved mongrel. Jumble regarded the next door garden as his own property. It would be impossible to keep him out of it. He found Jumble engaged in investigating the dustbin, fastened a piece of string to his collar and led him, thus secured,

down the passage that joined the back garden to the
"Tradesmen's Entrance". Jumble, resenting the
ignominy of being led on a piece of string, or indeed of
being led at all, resisted so strenuously that he could only
be dragged in a sitting position. He allowed himself to be
dragged in this position for some distance, then made a
sudden spirited resistance that took William by surprise
and threw him off his balance. It happened that one
boundary of the passage was formed by a blank,
windowless wall of the next house. At the foot of it was a
narrow, sunless border in which nothing would grow.
His father had long ago abandoned it to nature, and
nature had planted it with a rich profusion of docks,
nettles, and similar vegetation.

William's unpremeditated descent onto this border
had disturbed a thick cluster of nettles and had revealed
something in the wall behind them. He sat up and began
eagerly to examine it. Jumble sat by him and wagged his
stumpy tail in token of forgiveness. . . . A tiny aperture
with iron bars. A sort of ventilation hole.

He tugged at it with all his might. At last two rusty bars
came out. He put his eye close to the hole and looked
about. The ground sloped downward from the front of
the house to the back, and the ventilation hole evidently
ventilated a cellar beneath the ground floor of the next
house.

William's eyes gleamed. Here was his revenge ready
to hand. All he had to do now was to find a dead cat,
drop it down into the cellar, and await results. Suddenly
he noticed some wires near the opening along the cellar
wall. He tried to slip his hand in to touch them, but the
hole was too small. He took up the stick that he had been
carrying in his hand when he fell—William carried sticks
as naturally as most people wear clothes—and gave the

wires an exploratory probe. Immediately there came the sound of a bell jangling in the kitchen regions, then the front door was opened and after a few moments shut again with a bang expressive of intense irritation. William's lips parted in a seraphic smile. There was no need of dead cats. . . .

He rearranged the group of nettles over the ventilator, tied Jumble to the drain-pipe near the side door, and went into the kitchen, where his mother was taking advantage of the cook's afternoon out to make a cake.

"Mother," he said, assuming a vacant look that was meant to suggest extreme guilelessness, "I'd like to have a little garden of my own. May I?"

Mrs. Brown put down the currant tin and stared at him in amazement.

"But, *William*," she said, "I've offered you one over and over again, and you've always said you hated gardening, and the time you had one because your godmother promised you a shilling if you would, you never did a *thing* to it, and it got so choked with weeds that your father took it away from you."

"Yes, I know," admitted William shamelessly, "but that was a long time ago when I was quite different to what I am now. I've changed a lot since then. I'm quite different now to what I was then."

"You don't seem to have changed in any other way," said his mother, "you're just as careless and untidy and noisy and——"

"Yes, I know," interrupted William impatiently, "I mean, I've changed about gardens. I mean, I feel quite different about having a little garden of my own. I *want* to have a little garden of my own."

"But you won't take care of it," said Mrs. Brown.

"Yes, I will," said William, "I bet I'll always be out

there lookin' after it. You wait and see."

"You weren't when you had a garden before," said Mrs. Brown.

"No, but I keep telling you," said William, "I've changed since then. I'm quite different now to what I was then."

"Well, ask the gardener about it when he comes on Monday."

"No," said William, "I want to start gardening now. I don't want to wait till Monday."

Mrs. Brown was puzzled but gradually her native optimism came to her aid, and she took him round the garden, offering him suitable plots of land. William rejected them all.

"No," he said, "that's not the sort of piece I want."

"Well, what sort of piece *do* you want?" said Mrs. Brown at last in despair.

William appeared to notice for the first time the overgrown strip of border in the passage between the two houses.

"I'd like a piece of that," he said with enthusiasm, "I think that would make a jolly nice garden."

"*William!*" gasped Mrs. Brown amazed. "You know it gets no sun at all, and it's *choked* with weeds. Your father let it go because nothing would grow on it."

"Well, I like it," said William, "it's just the sort of garden I want."

"It will mean *days* of work to get it into order," said his mother. "All those weeds will have to be taken up."

"I know," said William unctuously, "that's why I want it. I want to have to work hard. I think it'll do me good."

Mrs. Brown, too much mystified to protest, assigned the piece of land to him and returned to her cake making.

In her letter to her husband that evening she wrote:

"William has asked for a piece of ground in the garden to make a little garden. He's always refused to have a garden before, you remember. I think that it's a very good sign and that it means he's beginning to appreciate the beauty of nature. . . ."

Robert, hearing of the idea, was contemptuous.

"I bet you sixpence," he said, "that he doesn't work more than five minutes on it. I know the little devil."

But evidently Robert did not know the little devil. All evening William knelt by his garden working patiently. A close observer might have noticed that his "work", though giving an appearance of great activity, was curiously unmethodical. He made a great show of pulling up weeds and digging the earth with a trowel, but little actual progress appeared to result from it. The close observer would have also noticed that, though he seemed to be working chiefly round the big clump of nettles in the middle of the bed, he did not even attempt to uproot them. During the time that he was at work upon his garden the bell rang in the next house six times. The first three times the maid went to it and reported to her master that there was no one there. The next two times the master of the house went himself to the door to answer it. The sixth time the master of the house hid behind the door with his stick and leapt out ferociously as soon as the bell sounded, hurling himself upon the imaginary culprit with such violence that he over-balanced and fell down the front door steps. He then proceeded to search the garden, thrusting his stick into the bushes and going on hands and knees to examine the recesses of the hedge. Meanwhile William worked on peacefully in his little garden.

The next morning he was at work again directly after breakfast. Mrs. Brown watched him proudly from the dining-room window.

"It's the greatest sign of improvement that I've seen in William for a long time," she said to Robert. "I'm sure his father will be glad to hear of it. After all, there can't be much wrong with a boy who's as fond of gardening as William seems to be now, and who deliberately chooses the most difficult piece of the whole garden, and works away at it with a will as William's doing."

Robert snorted contemptuously.

"If he *does* take to gardening," he said, "he'll pinch people's stuff for miles round and probably land us all in jail. At least," he added with heavy sarcasm, "if I know anything about him."

But their attention was distracted by an amazing spectacle. Major Bryant was, as usual, running down the road to the station to catch his train. Just as he had passed the next door house, the new neighbour leapt out with a stick, pursued him for some distance down the road, and finally fell upon him furiously. Major Bryant had been a heavyweight champion in his younger days, and he had lost little of his skill. In a few moments Mrs. Brown and Robert were gazing open-mouthed at the sight of the new neighbour climbing out of the ditch, then staggering homeward with his collar gaping open and his tie a crumpled rag beneath one ear.

When Mrs. Brown went out to tell William to get ready for school, he was still on his knees engaged in cultivating his little plot of land.

"It's time to get ready for school, dear," said Mrs. Brown. "What's that stick for?"

"What stick?" said William innocently.

"The one you've got in your hand."

"Oh, *that* one," said William. "Yes, I see. I didn't know you meant that one at first. Yes, I see . . . that stick. Oh, that's the stick I'm going to use to tie my plants up with."

"But you haven't got any plants."

"No, I know I haven't," said William, "but I thought I'd better have a stick ready for when I have."

"But what are you doing with it now?"

"Oh, now," temporised William. "Oh, I see what you mean . . . now. Yes, well, what I'm using it for now is this: I put it in the ground to mark the next piece of earth I've got to dig up, and when I've got to it I move it on to the next."

"Oh," said Mrs. Brown. She was thinking that William's method of gardening was rather strange, but then his method of doing everything was rather strange, so it did not really surprise her. "Well, it's time you went to get ready for school now, dear."

William got ready for school, leaving instructions that Jumble was not to be released.

During school his thoughts were busy. The incident of the next door neighbour and Major Bryant had opened new and exciting vistas before his eyes. After all, it was better that a revenge should not be too limited in its scope. William had many enemies of long standing in the village who might be included in this little effort. The masters found him unusually well-behaved that morning, if a little denser even than usual.

"Do you never listen to a word I say?" asked the history master.

"No, sir," said William politely, then hastily corrected it to "Yes, sir."

The mathematical master, who disliked William

"DO YOU NEVER LISTEN TO A WORD I SAY?" ASKED THE HISTORY
MASTER.

intensely and gave him frequent proofs of his dislike,
ordered him to stay in an hour after school. William
received the sentence with unusual meekness and with a
gleam of anticipatory pleasure in his eye.

He set to work again upon his garden as soon as he

returned home. Jumble sat near him occasionally thumping the ground with his tail in order to convey to William that he understood and approved his plan. As William worked, he cast frequent glances at the side gate, through which he could see whoever passed along the road. Soon he espied the figure of the mathematical master, ambling slowly along on his evening "constitutional". He busied himself energetically with his gardening operations, moving the stick from the spot of ground into which he had planted it. Hardly had the mathematical master passed the next door gate, when the new tenant came rushing down the drive and hurled himself upon him. William, hanging over the gate, was a delighted spectator of the ensuing struggle, in which the mathematical master distinctly came off worse.

William, of course, had not remained unsuspected. On several occasions when the bell rang, the neighbour, finding no one on the doorstep, had rushed to the gate of William's garden and glared down the passage at the small figure engaged so industriously upon its gardening operations; but it would not have been humanly possible for anyone, however agile, to have got from the front door step of the next house to that part of the garden in the time that had elapsed between the ringing of the bell and the discovery of William's industriously working form. William was too much of an artist to overdo things. The bell did not ring continuously. He waited always till the household next door should have settled down again to its various occupations before he made the next interruption. Several innocent callers were surprised to be greeted by the master of the house, who sprang out upon them brandishing a stick. The Vicar dropped a notice into the letter-box, rang the bell, then went away, and was stupefied to find himself pursued, seized by the collar and shaken furiously by his new parishioner, who at the same time announced his intention of dragging him off then and there to the police station on a charge of ringing bells and running away.

With great dignity the Vicar explained what had happened. The householder examined his letter-box and found the notice. The Vicar departed, straightening his crumpled collar and coldly stating that if he had not been a Minister of the Church he would certainly have brought an action for assault.

Growing more and more daring, William next rang the bell under the very eyes of the village policeman who, passing slowly down the road on his beat, had stopped to watch William's gardening activities. The enraged householder rushed out. To William's disappointment he did not fall upon the policeman—an old enemy of William's. He merely stated his case and asked the policeman if he had seen anyone come out of the gate. The policeman, whose life was rather a dull one, was deeply interested in the situation. No, he had seen no one. It would have been that young Brown without doubt, only, as it happened, he'd been at the Browns' gate for quite a time, and young Brown hadn't come out of the garden at all. He was doing a bit of gardening— queer thing for him, but still there it was—and hadn't moved from it for the last five minutes. So it must be someone else. And the policeman could take his oath that no one had come out, either. The culprit must be hiding in the garden. Together the policeman and the householder searched the garden, beating through the bushes and examining the hedge.

"Must have been hidin' somewhere near the gate and slipped out as we were lookin' over the other part," was the policeman's verdict. "If we can't find who did it," he went on confidentially, "we'll manage to put it onto young Brown. He's capable of it all right even if he didn't do it, and I've always wanted to get hold of something like this against him."

William, whose ears were sharper than the policeman realised, girded up his mental loins for the fight. No quarter was to be shown on either side.

His first step was to ask his mother to bring her sewing into the garden, and sit by him while he gardened. The request was unprecedented, and Mrs. Brown displayed some natural astonishment.

"But why, dear?" she said.

"Just for company," said William. "Just cause I'd—I'd like to have you near me while I did my garden."

Mrs. Brown was deeply touched. William had always seemed to her to be sadly lacking in that pretty affectionateness that makes some children so attractive. As a toddler he had invariably answered "Villum" when she asked him whom he loved best in all the world. She would always remember in future that he had asked her to come out to sit near him while he worked in his little garden. She brought out her chair and put it near him on the small path. Jumble placed himself between them. He was growing bored with William's gardening, and settling his head on his paw was soon asleep, twitching and growling softly as he chased rabbits in his sleep.

The bell rang in the next house five times during the next hour, and five times the master of the house rushed out to find no one there but the policeman, who had just passed the gate on his beat. On each occasion the two conferred together and looked down the passage to where William was working on his garden plot near his mother's basket chair. It would be impossible, of course, to "put it onto" William, when his mother was there to

THE POLICEMAN WRENCHED HIMSELF FREE SUFFICIENTLY TO RAISE HIS WHISTLE TO HIS LIPS.

bear witness that he had not even moved from the garden.

But the neighbour's manner was growing short and curt, and the gaze he fixed on the policeman was beginning to be one of deep suspicion.

Mrs. Brown's eyes were fixed on her mending, and

MRS. BROWN HEARD THE TUMULT AND RUSHED TO THE FENCE. FROM BEHIND HER A CRY OF AGONY BLENDED WITH THE POLICE-MAN'S WHISTLE.

her thoughts on the next day's menu, so she paid little attention to William's gardening. Once, however, she raised her head as if to listen and remarked: "The bell next door seems to be ringing a good deal." William emerged from his nettle clump to reply absently: "Is it?"

On the sixth occasion when, roused by the furious ringing of the bell, the neighbour came out to find no one in sight but the policeman, he fell upon him furiously.

"It's *you* all the time," he shouted. "It's *you* . . . *you* . . . *you*."

He emphasised his words with the stick upon the policeman's majestic person. The policeman wrenched himself free sufficiently to raise his whistle to his lips.

Mrs. Brown, summoned to the gate by the tumult, watched the scene with open-mouthed amazement.

From behind her a shrill cry of agony blended with the notes of the policeman's whistle.

William, unable to contain his jubilation, had turned a somersault into the middle of the clump of nettles.

*   *   *

William's father had returned from abroad. He sat enjoying his favourite chair and his favourite pipe.

"How's William gone on while I've been away?" he asked his wife. "Has he been good?"

"Oh, yes, *quite* good," said Mrs. Brown. "He wanted a garden of his own so I gave him a piece and he worked *very* hard on it for some days, then seemed suddenly to tire of it. I was rather disappointed, but"—she sighed—"one can't expect old heads on young shoulders, I suppose."

"What piece did you give him?" said her husband.

"That bit by the other house—the one you've given up."

Mr. Brown went over to the window and looked at the weed-infested strip.

"He doesn't seem to have done much to it," he commented.

"Oh, but he must have done, dear," said his wife, "he worked on it for *hours* before he suddenly tired of it."

"I see the next house is To Let again," said her husband, returning to his chair.

"Oh, *yes*," said Mrs. Brown. "That was quite an excitement. He was summoned for assaulting a policeman and fined. He said that someone had rung his door bell and run away, and he thought it was the policeman, and the policeman said that that couldn't be true, because he'd been on the road all the time and no one had gone into the gate. They nearly charged him with perjury as well. I'm not sorry he's gone. He was very rude to me."

"How was he rude to you?"

"I called, and he sent back my cards torn up. However, Robert went round and made him apologise."

"Perhaps William had been annoying him."

"Oh, no, dear. William was *quite* well behaved all the time he was there. I told you. He got this craze for gardening and hardly stirred out of the garden."

They looked at William. He was standing at the window that looked on the front road, obviously deaf to all they were saying. So intently was he gazing at the road that Mrs. Brown crossed over to the window to see whatever there was to be seen.

There was, however, nothing to be seen. The road was quite empty.

She could not know, of course, that William was watching his army of bandits with flying of banners and flourish of trumpets marching down from Ringers Hill to take up their quarters again in the empty house.

Chapter 6

Mrs. Bott's Hat

"I've always wanted to be something excitin'," said William, "and that's what I'm goin' to be."

"What?" said his Outlaws.

"I'm goin' to be like this man," said William; "this man in this book I've just been reading."

"Yes, but what *about* him?" said Ginger.

"I keep tryin' to *tell* you, but you keep int'ruptin'," said William impatiently. "I tell you I want to do like this man did. It'd be jolly excitin', an' it's ever so long since I did anythin' really excitin'."

"You made your geyser explode last week," Douglas gently reminded him.

"Well, I don't call that *really* excitin'," said William, "not excitin' like the things this man in the book did. Well, I'm goin' to start doin' them to-day."

"Doin' what?" said his Outlaws.

William sighed.

"I keep tellin' you. You won't *listen*. You will keep int'ruptin'. I want to do somethin' excitin' same as this man in this book did."

"Yes, but *what* did he do?" shouted the Outlaws.

"If you'd stop int'ruptin' for one *minute*," said William sternly, "I'd tell you. You keep int'ruptin' and *int'ruptin'*. This man stole things."

"It's wrong to steal things," said Douglas piously.

"Yes, I know, but it's only wrong to steal things if you keep them for yourself."

"Well, we tried stealing things for the poor, and it wasn't a success."

"Well, this man in this book didn't steal things for the poor."

"Who did he steal them for then?"

"He didn't steal them for anyone. He just got someone to bet him he wouldn't steal something, and then he stole it just for the daringness of it and then put it back. And putting the things back was just as dangerous as stealing them. Well, that's what I'm goin' to do. I'm sick of nothin' excitin' happenin' for days an' *days*. You've got to fix on somethin' to bet me I won't steal an' then I'm goin' to steal it an' bring it to show you an' put it back an' it's goin' to be jolly dangerous an' excitin' same as it was in this book. Now you think of somethin' to bet me I won't steal. . . ."

The Outlaws brightened. The Christmas holidays were dragging somewhat. The weather, while debarring them from the activities that made the summer holidays so enjoyable, failed to provide compensating winter occupation. It had rained incessantly till to-day. To-day was fine, but cold, dark, and vaguely depressing. Therefore the Outlaws brightened at the thought of William's new career.

"Yes," said Ginger judicially. "I think it's a jolly fine idea. Well, you go away a minute an' we'll think of somethin'."

William wandered over to the other side of the field till a cry of "Ready" recalled him. He returned to the three Outlaws.

"You're not to send me to steal anything miles and miles away like somethin' in the Tower of London or anythin' like that," he said, "because it's too far for me to go an' I'm not goin' to waste any money on train fares."

"No, it isn't that," Ginger reassured him. "It isn't anythin' in The Tower of London."

"What is it then?" asked William.

"It's Mrs. Bott's Sunday hat," said Ginger.

Mrs. Bott's Sunday hat was a well-known feature of the local landscape. It was large and plentifully trimmed with ostrich feathers. Mrs. Bott's husband had made a fortune by his sauce, and, while Mrs. Bott had acquired many of the tastes of the class into which the fortune had raised her, in millinery her taste remained true to the immortal type of Hampstead Heath.

"Mrs.——" began William indignantly. "A big thing like *that!* Why, I couldn't put it in my pocket or—or anywhere. I nat'rally meant something I could put in my pocket."

"Well, you didn't say so," said Ginger triumphantly, "an' we've chosen Mrs. Bott's Sunday hat."

"I *can't* steal Mrs. Bott's Sunday hat."

"You can't steal anythin', that's what it is."

"I can. I can steal anythin' but *that*. A *hat!* I never heard of anyone stealin' a *hat*. How'm I goin' to get it back even if I steal it—a big thing like that? You dunno how to choose things to steal."

"Well, we're not goin' to choose anythin' else," retorted Ginger; "we've chosen Mrs. Bott's Sunday hat an' we're not goin' to change. You're frightened of Mrs. Bott, that's what it is."

"I'm not."

"You are."

"I'm not."

"You are."

"I'm not."

"All right—steal her Sunday hat then if you aren't frightened of her."

"All right," said William, stung to valour by their taunts, "I will. Just to *show* you. You stay here an' I'll steal it an' bring it to you an' put it back again. I'm not frightened of *anyone*."

The Outlaws cheered enthusiastically, and William set off with his best swagger down the road.

His swagger died down as he reached the Hall gates, and he entered them furtively, keeping well in the shadow of the shrubs that bordered the drive. When he came in sight of the house, he betook himself entirely to cover, and did not emerge till he was exactly opposite the front door, when he cautiously raised his head from the middle of a rhododendron bush and surveyed the prospect. The large, balconied bedroom with the bay window must be Mrs. Bott's. His quarry was presumably there in a wardrobe or drawer or hat box. There was no convenient drain-pipe near the window, and, in any case, he could hardly have climbed it in broad daylight and in full view of the whole garden. He was just considering without much hope the plan of calling boldly at the front door and saying that he had come to look at the gas meter or tune the piano (a trick often played by the hero of his book), when the front door opened, and Mrs. Bott came out wearing her best coat and the Sunday hat secured by a large veil. William was too much startled to withdraw his head immediately, and for a minute Mrs. Bott and William stared at each other in silence. Then Mrs. Bott moved off down the drive to a spot where her head gardener was engaged in superintending the planting of a display of bulbs.

"Binks," she said majestically, "I don't like carved

bushes, so don't start doing it here."

"I beg your pardon, madam," said the bewildered Binks.

"I say I don't like carved bushes," she said. "I think it's unnatural. I like a bush to be a bush same as nature made it. You ought to have asked me before you started doing it."

"Doing what, madam?"

"Carving bushes. I've just told you. You've started carving bushes opposite the house, and I don't like it."

"I still don't understand you, madam," said Binks with all the majesty of a gardener who commanded four under-gardeners.

"Well, surely to goodness you know what carved bushes are, Binks?" said Mrs. Bott impatiently.

"Are you referring to topiary work, madam?" said Binks.

"You can call it what you like," said Mrs. Bott, "I call it carved bushes. Bushes carved into shapes—balls and animals and suchlike. And I won't have it. It's unnatural."

"There is no topiary work in this garden, madam," said Binks coldly.

"Well, I may be short-sighted," said Mrs. Bott with spirit, "I know I *am* short-sighted, but I can see when a bush has got a big ball sticking out in the middle of it, and balls don't come into bushes by themselves. They've got to be carved. Someone's started carving those bushes, and it's got to be stopped, and that's all I've got to say, and I'm not going to argue over it any more."

With that she swept off down the drive towards the gate, leaving Binks gazing after her motionless, his mouth wide open.

William, who, concealed now in a laurel bush, had

listened to the conversation with a good deal of relief, followed her under cover to the gate, and then set off behind her down the road, his eyes fixed longingly on the concoction of nodding plumes that crowned the small, stout figure. As he walked, various plans for the possession of the prize revolved in his mind, only to be dismissed one after another. He might demand it highwayman fashion, saying that he had a colleague in hiding, armed with a pistol, who would shoot at once if she did not give it up to him. He might approach her and beg it from her on behalf of some imaginary old woman who could not go out because she was too poor to buy a hat. He might hurry on before her in the ditch, climb a tree, and bend down to twitch it off her head as she passed. It was just as he was reluctantly dismissing the last plan as impracticable that he realised with surprise that Mrs. Bott was entering the gate of his own house. She knocked at the door and was admitted, evidently as an expected guest. William did not take much interest in his mother's social engagements, but he suddenly remembered having heard his mother say that she was expecting a visitor to tea. The visitor, then, was Mrs. Bott. He entered behind her and hovered about in the hall as his mother came forward.

"Would you like to come upstairs and take your hat off?" said his mother after greeting her guest.

"Well, dear," replied Mrs. Bott, "it *would* be rather nice. I mean, I always find a hat makes one's head ache, don't you? So heavy, aren't they, always, hats. It's very nice of you to think of it. Some people don't. . . ."

William waited in the hall, pretending to be engaged in looking for something on the hat stand, till Mrs. Bott and his mother came downstairs. Mrs. Bott was drawing her fingers through her very golden hair.

"You've simply got to be all eyes," Mrs. Bott was saying. "The minute you turn your back they're up to some tricks. Carving the bushes they started to-day. If I'd not put my foot down the place would have been full of birds and animals and set-outs like that by the time I got home. Unnatural I call it. I like a bush to be a bush same as nature made it."

Still talking, she entered the drawing-room and the door was closed.

"YOU'VE SIMPLY GOT TO BE ALL EYES," MRS. BOTT WAS SAYING.
"THE MINUTE YOU TURN YOUR BACK THEY'RE UP TO SOME TRICKS."

William slipped quickly upstairs to his mother's bed-room and stood frowning thoughtfully at the enormous concoction that lay upon the bed. Mrs. Bott's visit to his mother had seemed at first to make everything gloriously, miraculously simple, but suddenly he wasn't sure.

It would be impossible to carry this creation through the village street to the old barn. Someone would be sure to recognise it and stop him. Impossible even to wrap it in paper. It was too large and feathery. It would refuse in any circumstances to form a "parcel". His brow cleared as a bright idea struck him. He would slip on hat and coat and veil and walk to the barn in them. Anyone meeting him would think he was Mrs. Bott and pass by without suspicion or surprise. He would return from the old barn long before it was time for Mrs. Bott to go home, slip up to the bedroom again, and replace the hat and coat on the bed without anyone's having discovered their disap-pearance. It was all perfectly simple. William put on the coat and hat and tied the veil tightly round the hat and under his chin. He was, of course, a little shorter than Mrs. Bott, and the coat came right down to his shoes. Still—the hat came low over his forehead and the veil was very thick so that little of his face could be seen, and to a very casual observer he would certainly suggest Mrs. Bott. He crept cautiously downstairs to the hall, then stood still and listened intently. The drawing-room door was slightly ajar, and from it came the sound of Mrs. Bott's voice sustaining its inevitable monologue. "All right for shows and suchlike," it was saying, "but in an ordinary garden I like a bush to be a bush same as nature made it, an' I told him so straight."

From the kitchen came the subdued sounds of tea preparations. He crept to the side door and looked out.

There was no one in the road. He opened the door very silently and slipped out of the house.

It happened that, just as he opened the side door, the housemaid opened the door of the kitchen and caught sight of his retreating figure. Open mouthed, she went into the hall and, pressing her face to the glass panes, watched him disappear into the road. Then she put her eye to the hinge of the drawing-room door to gaze at the figure of Mrs. Bott seated in an armchair talking expansively. She returned to the kitchen as if in a dream.

"Well," said the cook, "where's them silver spoons?"

"I've not got 'em," said the housemaid. "I've seen a vishun."

"Well, never mind vishuns," said the cook, "it was the silver spoons you went for."

"I've seen the hastral body of Mrs. Bott walking out of the house while her earthly body sits in the drawing-room talking to the mistress."

"Well, you'll be talking to the mistress soon," said the cook, "if you don't hurry up and get them spoons from the dining-room."

"Aren't you interested in vishuns?" said the housemaid, stung by the cook's attitude.

"No, I'm not," said the cook, "but I'm interested in having this tea on time, and I want them silver spoons."

The housemaid tossed her head, affronted.

"I can tell you my New Thought Circle 'll take it a bit different," she said.

"They can take it how they like," said the cook, "so long as you get them silver spoons."

Meantime William had passed safely through the village street, which happened to be empty. He had now only a few yards to go to the stile that led to the old barn.

The adventure was practically at an end. It had been, on the whole, a little tame and disappointing. It was just as he came to this conclusion that he saw the figure of Mr. Bott walking down the road to meet him. In panic-stricken flight he plunged down a side lane and looked around for a place of hiding. A few yards down the lane stood an unattended trade lorry.

William climbed quickly into this and drew a piece of sacking over his head. After a few moments he heard steps coming down the lane and approaching the lorry. Mr. Bott, of course, coming to investigate the strange and sudden flight of his wife. . . . William crouched beneath the sack, hardly daring to breathe.

Suddenly there came the sound of an engine starting up, and, before William realised what had happened, the lorry set off with a jerk, and he found himself travelling down the road at thirty miles an hour. William cautiously emerged from his sack. The steps had belonged to the lorry driver. Mr. Bott, who was even more short-sighted than his wife, was placidly continuing his way through the village. The back of the lorry driver was broad and muscular—so broad and muscular that William decided not to make his presence known at once, but to wait till the lorry stopped and then depart from it as unobtrusively as he had entered it. Meantime, he sat up and looked about him. On the lorry were several baskets of apples. William thought he might as well take whatever compensations the situation offered, so he lay back comfortably against the end of the lorry, raising his veil, and began to munch apples and watch the countryside flash by. The lorry seemed to be going rather a long way. William was already considering the possibility of it being on its way to Scotland, when it stopped suddenly at a small public-house.

William gathered himself together for flight, but it turned out that the lorry driver was not, after all, leaving his lorry. A man in his shirt-sleeves came out from the public-house carrying a glass of beer.

"Usual, I suppose, Jim?" he said, and stood talking to the lorry man while he drank it.

William, who was well out of their sight at the head of the lorry, continued to munch his apple. His attention soon wandered from their conversation—which was very dull and concerned the prospects of various horses in various races—and he began to survey the landscape, trying without success to discover any familiar features. Suddenly there was a lull in the conversation, and William turned round with a start to find that the man in shirt-sleeves had walked round to the side of the lorry and was staring at him with amazement.

"What yer lookin' at?" said the driver.

"Brought yer misses along ter-day, I see," said the man. "Wouldn't she like a glass of somethin'?"

There was an abrupt movement on the driver's seat, and William looked up to find a large red face glaring down at him furiously. Without a moment's hesitation William leapt from the lorry, and, gathering his voluminous coat about him, set off at a quick run down the road. Once out of sight and finding that he was not pursued, he stopped running and again looked about him. The road forked at the point where he had stopped, and one fork seemed to lead to a village. William decided to follow this. In the village he could find out how far he was from home. He pulled down his veil, arranged his coat and hat, and set off jauntily towards the village. William's spirit was not one that yields easily to defeat, and he still had hopes of winning his bet. When he had walked some way down the road, he heard the sound of the lorry, and turned to see it taking the other fork of the road. The lorry driver shook his fist in William's direction as he vanished from sight, and William put out his tongue behind his veil. In the village he approached an old man who sat on a seat outside a public-house, and, adopting the shrill falsetto voice with which in their games he impersonated the damsel whom the other Outlaws had to rescue, asked him the name of the village and the means of getting back to his home. The old man, who was deaf and short-sighted, noticed nothing peculiar in William's voice or appearance, and readily gave the required information, adopting on his side a quavering voice, and intimating that he suffered from a chronic complaint for which the doctor had prescribed beer, but that he had spent his last penny on food for a sick friend. William, not being the rich old lady of the old man's hopes, merely grunted on receiving this information, and busied himself in drawing up his coat to get to his trouser pocket (a proceeding that shocked the old man inexpressibly) and count his money. Yes, he had enough money to get home by the 'bus. . . . There was, however, half an hour to wait. William hated waiting. He sat down on the seat by the old man (who was still glaring at him, outraged by his lack of womanly modesty) and drummed his heels in the dust.

He waited for what seemed to him quite half an hour and found, on looking at the church clock, that only two minutes had gone. He then amused himself for some time by throwing stones at a tree across the road, increasing the horror and disgust of the old man, finally practising a long jump in the middle of the road—a proceeding that sent the old man hobbling quickly homewards. ("Out of Bedlam, her is . . . out of

Bedlam.") Having practised long jumps for what seemed half an hour, William again looked at the church clock and found that only two more minutes had passed. It was just then that the unmistakable sound of a country fair came to his ears. He stood still and listened. William could never resist a country fair. He hastily felt in his pockets again. Yes, he had a few coppers beyond what would be needed for his 'bus fare. He could have a ride on the roundabout, and still be back in time to catch the 'bus home. Adjusting his hat and veil (for it still seemed less conspicuous to be a lady in a hat and coat than to be a boy carrying a lady's hat and coat), he set off down the road in the direction of the sounds and soon reached the fair ground. Already a dense crowd was streaming into it. William joined the crowd and made his way quickly to the nearest roundabout. He climbed upon it (remembering to sustain his character by sitting sideways) and surrendered himself to bliss. So lost was he to the ecstasy of the up-and-down-and-round-and-round movement that he failed to notice that he was attracting a good deal of attention. The large crowd that surrounded the merry-go-round was in fact occupying itself solely with watching him. Interested smiles followed his circular progress and his frequent reappearance at every part of the circle. Fingers pointed at him and voices cried: "Look, there she is. There—coming round again!"

Still unaware of this, William, having spent his last available penny, descended decorously from the roundabout, and began to make his way towards the gate again. It was then that he realised with surprise and horror that he was walking between serried ranks of interested spectators, who made way for him, pointing him out to each other. "Look, there she is . . . she's just been on the roundabout."

The way that the crowd made for him did not lead to the exit. It led to a tent—a tent that bore a large notice: "Mr. & Mrs. Tom Thumb. Entrance 2d. 6 o'clock prompt." William had no option but to take it. He walked slowly and with a sinking of the heart towards the tent. . . .

"Well, I shan't pay 2d. to see her now," a woman said loudly as he passed her, "and I don't think much of her either."

William hesitated at the tent door, but the crowd that lined his path had closed up behind him and was pressing him on. He entered the tent door apprehensively. What chiefly worried him was the "Entrance 2d". Should the entrance fee be demanded of him, he would not have enough money left for his 'bus fare. He had a vague idea of hiding just inside the tent door till the crowd had dispersed, but there was no room to hide inside the tent door. It opened immediately into a sawdust-covered interior with a small platform at one end. A mirror hung from the pole that supported the tent, and in front of this stood a little woman about William's size arranging a hat that was, like William's, large and feathered. She wheeled round as William appeared and stood staring at him in amazement. Then her amazement vanished, and she came across to him, smiling a coy, bright, affected smile and holding out a small hand.

"How are you, dear? From Belson's, aren't you?"

William realised that if he was from Belson's he would be welcomed as a friend and no entrance fee demanded, so he decided to be from Belson's.

"Yes," he said in his shrill falsetto voice.

"Of course, dear. Just for a moment it gave me quite a start seeing you standing there, then I knew, of course, you must be from Belson's. Funny you an' me 've never met before, isn't it, dear? An' so often we've just followed each other. Last time we were at Marleigh you'd moved on the day before. People said: 'Why, Belson's Mrs. Tom Thumb was here only yesterday. And as like as two peas to you, dear.' Of course, our strong man knows Belson's strong man quite well. It was him I sent the message to you by. It was good of you to come over at once, dear. I suppose you don't open till to-night?"

"No," said William in his shrill falsetto.

"We don't open till six. I tell you what, dear. Suppose I walk over to Belson's with you. I'd love to see it. It's so seldom that one can see any show except one's own, and it's apt to make one a bit narrow. It's in the glebe field over at Marston, isn't it? I could easily be back by six. How's things going with you, dear? Our strong man says that Belson's elastic woman is nothing compared to ours, but that his mermaid beats ours hollow. I told the boss ours ought to have a fresh tail *months* ago. It drops scales whenever she moves, and a thing like that lets the whole show down. Well, dear, what about it? Shall I walk back to Belson's with you?"

"Yes," shrilled William, wondering helplessly where the adventure was going to end.

"My hubby's just gone to have a drink with the fire swallower," continued Mrs. Tom Thumb. "I don't expect he'll be back till six. . . . Well, shall we start, dear? Out this way behind the tent. So many crowds at the front. Living in the limelight has its drawbacks, as I'm sure you've found out, dear. Sometimes I get sick of crowds and admiration." She preened her small figure complacently. "But there—we've got to put up with it same as royalty. . . . Here we are. Through this gate to the road. It's only a mile or two, dear, isn't it?"

"Yes," squeaked William, who felt as if in the grip of a nightmare.

There seemed nothing for it but to walk down the road with the garrulous little lady. She was glancing at him critically as they walked.

"Now, you mustn't mind me saying it, dear, but I'm surprised to find you like you are. I was told you were as dainty and elegant as me, but—well, you seem a bit clumsy somehow. You mustn't be annoyed, dear, because we can't be all in the front rank, as it were, can we? Well, it stands to reason that we can't, doesn't it? To me you seem made a bit clumsy, though I'll grant you you're short. Perhaps I'm over particular. Of course, the *Mudbury Chronicle* called me 'a gem of miniature perfection,' so I've probably got higher standards than what some people have——"

She stopped suddenly, and gave a gasp, staring at William in indignant horror.

For William had unthinkingly drawn up the coat again to get his handkerchief from his trousers pocket, and had revealed the stalwart nether limbs of a schoolboy clad in grey tweed shorts.

Mrs. Tom Thumb's small countenance turned to an angry purple. Her eyes blazed furiously. "A *boy!*" she screamed. "A fraud, a cheat, that's what you are. I'll show you up. I'll show Belson's up. I'll tell the whole place what you are. Cheating the public all these years! And people saying you were as good as me—me that's a gem of miniature perfection, you little hound, you!"

With these words the enraged lady sprang at William as if to shake or scratch him. William dodged and set off at a brisk run down the road, pursued for some distance by the gem of miniature perfection.

At the end of the road he stopped and turned round.

Mrs. Thumb had given up the chase and was now contenting herself with shaking a small fist at him and screaming abuse from half-way down the road. William turned the corner and looked about him apprehensively. There was nothing to be seen, however, but the 'bus that was just on the point of starting. He slipped a finger into each side of his mouth, emitted a piercing whistle, then

WILLIAM EMITTED A PIERCING WHISTLE, THEN RAN DOWN THE ROAD AND LEAPT UPON THE 'BUS.

ran down the road and leapt upon the 'bus under the
eyes of the amazed conductor.

*   *   *

William alighted from the 'bus at his own gate and
stood for a moment in the shadow of the hedge, again
looking cautiously around him. Through the drawing-
room window he could see Mrs. Bott's golden head and
fat, smiling face. She had evidently not yet discovered
the loss of her hat and coat. There was no one in the side
path. The side door was ajar. He could see the hall with
its rows of hooks. Most of them supported coats and hats
belonging to his family, but one was empty. The temp-
tation to relieve himself of his encumbrances without
further ceremony was irresistible. He went quickly up
the side walk and into the hall; there he slipped off hat,
coat, and veil, and was just in the act of hanging them
onto the hook when the house was filled with a strange
commotion. Cook ran out of the kitchen and pounded
upstairs, her large bulk moving with incredible speed.
With the same furious speed she pounded down again,
crying: "Oh, mam, the boiler's burst. . . . The water's
coming down through the ceiling in your bedroom. . . .
I heard a funny noise and went up to see and it was
that. . . . And it's all coming down through the ceiling.
. . . Oh, mam, oh, mam!"

Mrs. Brown, followed by Mrs. Bott, emerged from
the drawing-room and ran hastily upstairs. . . . Soon
they reappeared.

"Ring up the plumber, Cook," called Mrs. Brown, "and
put some pans on the floor to catch the water. . . ."

Suddenly she noticed William, who had been struck
motionless by amazement in the act of hanging up Mrs.
Bott's hat and coat.

"Oh, *William!*" said Mrs. Brown, "how *thoughtful* of you. . . . I think it was *splendid* of you, dear. Look, Mrs. Bott, he ran upstairs to rescue your hat and coat as soon as he heard the water. . . . You should have given the alarm at once, dear, but never mind. You saved Mrs. Bott's hat and coat, which is the main thing. I think it showed *great* thoughtfulness and presence of mind."

"OH, *WILLIAM!*" SAID MRS. BROWN, "HOW *THOUGHTFUL* OF YOU."

William hastily assumed an expression of thoughtfulness and presence of mind and wisely refrained from any comment on the situation.

Mrs. Bott, feeling that any extension of her visit would be an anti-climax, thanked William profusely, and took her leave. As soon as she had gone, Mr. Brown came home, and Mrs. Brown gave him a confused but excited account of what had happened.

"And, my dear, it was *pouring* through from the ceiling of our bedroom. The man's seeing to it now and cook's put pots and things all over the floor, but it's *soaked* the bed, and, my dear, I can't think *what* would have happened if William hadn't had the presence of mind to slip up and rescue her coat and hat as soon as he heard the sound of the dripping. My dear, Heaven only knows what that dreadful hat cost, and it would have been *ruined—ruined! And* the coat! It would have cost us *pounds* to replace them. It was really *splendid* of William to think of rescuing them, don't you think so, dear?"

"It certainly showed a bit more sense than I gave him credit for," said Mr. Brown, handing William a shilling before going upstairs to inspect the damage.

William set off to join his Outlaws. He walked with the swagger of one who had just performed a noble rescue. As he walked, his artist's mind was busy with the exploit—adjusting its details, making it more worthy of him.

The Outlaws were awaiting him at the old barn.

"Well?" they said eagerly.

"Well, I rescued her," said William. "The place was flooded. Flooded from top to bottom. An' she was upstairs an' no one could get to her an' she'd have been drowned in two seconds if I hadn't swum upstairs an' rescued her an' then swum downstairs again, holdin' her in my arms, an' I saved her life, an' by rights I ought to have a statue put up to me."

"Yes, but what about the *hat*?" said the Outlaws, who had heard too many stories of William's heroic exploits to be deeply impressed.

"I rescued her hat, too," said William, "and my father gave me a shilling."

"Yes, but you were going to *steal* it," the Outlaws reminded him vociferously.

William's mind travelled over the past to the adventure preceding the burst boiler.

"Oh, yes," he said, "I did steal it. I've been all over England in it."

"Never mind all over England," said Ginger sternly, "the bet was that you'd to bring it here for us to see."

"Oh, yes," said William, "I remember now. Well, I did steal the hat, but I forgot about bringin' it here. When I got back I was so sick of it that I jus' saw a hook in the hall an' didn't think of anything but jus' gettin' it hung up on it. I tell you I've been all over England in it. I've been on lorries an' performin' in fairs in it——"

"Oh, shut *up*," said Ginger, for William suffered from the drawback that attends a fertile imagination in that people seldom gave him credit for such details in his stories as happened to be true. "Shut up about lorries and fairs an' rubbish like that. You said you'd steal her hat and you didn't."

"I did."

"You didn't."

"I did, I tell you."

"Why didn't you bring it here, then?"

"I keep *telling* you, only you won't listen. I started out to bring it here, but I got all messed up in lorries an' fairs an' rescuing people from drownin' an' things like that."

"I don't believe you ever *did* steal it."

"Are you callin' me a liar?" said William, adopting a pugnacious attitude.

"Yes," said Ginger simply.

"All right," said William, and began to go through an elaborate process of taking off his coat and rolling up his sleeves with a good many unnecessary flourishes. Ginger did the same. . . . But just as they were squaring up to each other, Douglas, who was standing at the door of the barn, called out: "*Look!*"

They ran to the door of the barn.

From the dark sky small white flakes were beginning to fall, growing bigger and bigger.

"Snow!" shouted the Outlaws excitedly.

Forgetting everything else in the world, they leapt forth exultantly, holding out their hands to catch the falling flakes in eager competition as to which of them should make the first snowball.

Chapter 7

William and the Princess Goldilocks

It was Robert, William's elder brother, who took him to the pantomime, not because he wanted to take him there but because he had rashly promised to take him and William ruthlessly held him to the promise.

He had made the promise in a moment of weakness on a blazing summer day when a Christmas pantomime seemed as remote as the millennium. Robert and Ethel were giving a tennis party, and William's services as ball-boy had to be requisitioned for the afternoon. Robert had requisitioned them in the high-handed manner that he felt was due to his eight years seniority but on which he secretly placed little hope.

"And you," he had said imperiously, "will fetch the balls for us."

"Oh, will I?" said William.

"Yes, you will," said Robert firmly, thinking he might as well give the high-handed manner a good chance before he was driven to abandon it.

"Who's going to make me?" said William.

"I am," said Robert.

"All right," said William. "You make me then."

Robert was, of course, aware that it is difficult, if not impossible, to play an impressive game of tennis and at the same time force an unwilling younger brother to search for missing balls. Reluctantly he abandoned the high-handed manner.

"Now look here," he said, in a man-to-man tone of voice. "You wouldn't like to sit by and watch us looking for our own tennis balls, would you?"

"Yes, I would," said William, unmoved by the pathos of this picture.

Robert added a touch of indignation to his man-to-man manner.

"I'm sure you wouldn't like it to be said in the village that you'd simply sat by and let us fetch our own balls."

"Yes, I would," said William again. "Anyway, I wouldn't be sittin' by. I'd be out playin' with Ginger."

Robert gave a short laugh indicative of incredulity and disgust.

"My dear boy, you *surely* couldn't go out to play with a free mind, *knowing* that there was no one here to help us."

"Yes, I could," said William firmly and without hesitation.

There was a short silence. Both knew, of course, that William would eventually stay at home to be ball-boy for the tennis party. It was simply a question of conditions. William broke the silence.

"How much will you give me if I do it?" he said bluntly.

Robert smiled a superior smile. Not for worlds would he have admitted to William that his month's allowance was exhausted and that he was at the moment as penniless as William himself.

"Oh, we'll talk about that after the party," he said evasively.

"All right," said William. "And I'll be ball-boy after

the party."

"Don't be absurd," said Robert. "It's for the party we want you."

"Well then, how much are you going to give me for it?"

Robert gazed absently into the distance as if he were lost in profound thought and had forgotten William's presence. William, unimpressed by this manœuvre, waited stolidly for his answer. After some minutes, when it had become quite obvious that William did not intend to steal tactfully away leaving Robert to his meditation, Robert seemed to realise his presence with a start.

"Oh! You're still there, are you?" he said carelessly. "I was thinking of something else. . . . Well, it's arranged that you will be ball-boy, isn't it? You'd better be ready by three. We'll get a set going as soon as enough people turn up."

"Yes," said William. "And how much are you goin' to give me for it?"

Robert put his hands into his pockets with the air of one about to jingle coins then hastily withdrew them. William realised the situation. He realised, too, that, whether Robert gave him anything for his services or not, he would be compelled by his mother to be ball-boy for the tennis party. He hastened to extract some definite promise from Robert before his mother should be appealed to.

"Will you take me to the pantomime at Christmas?" he asked.

"Yes, certainly," said Robert, resuming his lofty manner. "And you'll be ready for work by three?"

"All right," agreed William.

During the months that followed an uneasy memory

of this promise occasionally visited Robert, but he consoled himself by the reflection that William had probably forgotten it, and carefully refrained from reminding him of it. To all appearances indeed William had forgotten it. He never mentioned it. Even when pantomimes were spoken of in his presence, he behaved as if the reference woke no chord of memory in his breast. For William, in the course of his eleven years, had garnered no small store of wisdom. He knew that Robert, who was passing through a high-brow stage, did not want to take him to the pantomime. And he knew that to remind Robert prematurely of his promise would be to risk having it annulled on the score of one of his many misdemeanours. Too often had William seen grown-ups extricate themselves from inconvenient obligations in that way. He bided his time till the last week of the Christmas holidays, then very neatly cornered the unsuspecting Robert.

"You're taking me to the pantomime to-morrow, aren't you, Robert?" he said casually.

"*What?*" exploded Robert.

"I said you were taking me to the pantomime to-morrow," said William, obligingly raising his voice.

Robert assumed an expression of blankness and surprise.

"Whenever did I say that?" he demanded.

Neither the blankness nor the surprise, however, were very convincing, and he had an uneasy suspicion that William had once more got the better of him.

"At your tennis party in the summer. For being ball-boy," explained William succinctly. "An' I go back to school next week an' to-morrow's the only day you aren't doin' anything before I go back an' you've got plenty of money 'cause father gave you your money yesterday, so you'll have to take me to-morrow to keep your promise."

Robert realised that he had been outwitted but made a desperate bid for escape.

"Oh, yes," he admitted casually; "but it depends, of course, on how you behave between now and to-morrow."

"All right," grinned William and performed the seemingly impossible feat of twelve hours' virtue by the simple means of absenting himself from his home except for meals and appearing at meals in a state of startling cleanliness whose achievement afforded him much secret amusement and triumph. No alternative was left to Robert but to take William to the pantomime. He did it without any unnecessary sociability, taking him straight there and straight back, sitting through the performance with an air of intense boredom and ostentatiously reading a volume of Tchehov's plays during the intervals. Whenever the comedians elicited a guffaw from him he covered the slip as quickly as possible by intensifying the pained aloofness of his expression.

To William the afternoon was one of unclouded bliss. He laughed at the comedians so uproariously that he thought once or twice that he must have broken a rib, he cheered the hero, he hissed the villain, he clapped and shouted applause long after every one around him had stopped. And he fell in love with Princess Goldilocks, the heroine.

Every smile she threw at the audience thrilled him, every tone of her voice was music to him. He could not help thinking that his passion was returned, for she seemed to smile directly at him, to speak to him alone. As he followed the crowd out of the theatre—Robert looking very stern lest anyone should suspect that he had secretly enjoyed the show—he felt that all the rest of his life must be devoted to her service. There was no time to be lost. He must woo and win her as soon as possible. He must overcome the villains who probably surrounded her in real life as well as in the play and give her a palace

**WILLIAM FELL IN LOVE WITH PRINCESS GOLDILOCKS. EVERY SMILE
SHE THREW AT THE AUDIENCE THRILLED HIM.**

AND SHE SEEMED TO SMILE DIRECTLY AT HIM, TO SPEAK TO HIM
ALONE.

and jewels as good as the ones the hero gave her in the last act. The knowledge that the hero was really a girl was a great comfort to him. She could not, he decided, be in love with the red-nosed comedian, or the bald-headed juggler, or the Baron who stammered, or the Boots who squinted, or the robber with the ferocious whiskers. The coast seemed to be left wonderfully and miraculously clear for him. He would have gone round to the stage door straight away to propose to her if Robert had not pulled him unceremoniously into the street and onto a 'bus. During the next few days William seemed to those around him to be strangely quiet and docile. They could not, of course, know that in reality he was engaged in desperate adventures—fighting armies of brigands single-handed, storming rocky strongholds, outwitting cunning villains, killing ferocious wild beasts. These adventures always terminated happily, and the rescued Princess Goldilocks flung herself into his arms sobbing out her gratitude and love.

So pleasant, indeed, were these adventures that at first they completely satisfied William. Then gradually he began to find them unconvincing. They left him exactly where he was before. He must betake himself to the sterner stuff of real life. After much consideration he decided to walk to London, make his way into her room at the theatre and ask her to marry him at once. He would take some food with him and as much money as he could extract from his mother. He was an optimist, but he was afraid it would not be very much. Wearing an expression of almost painful virtue, he entered the drawing-room where his mother and Ethel sat over the fire doing needlework.

"They say that an actress is staying at the Cedars," Ethel was saying as he entered.

"The Cedars?" said Mrs. Brown vaguely.

"Yes . . . that place in Marleigh they've turned into a hotel, you know. They've been advertising it a lot—old-fashioned Christmas and that sort of thing. She goes up every day to London for the show."

"What show is she in?" asked Mrs. Brown.

"A pantomime. The one that Robert took William to. She's Goldilocks or something."

"What's the matter, William?" said Mrs. Brown, turning to her younger son who stood in the doorway listening, his eyes and mouth wide open. "Do you want anything?"

"Oh, no," said William, quickly recovering himself. "No, I just looked in to see if you were all right."

"Why shouldn't we be all right, dear?" said Mrs. Brown, touched but slightly mystified.

But William had vanished. He was already on his way to Marleigh. Marleigh was five miles distant by road but two by the field path. William knew the big country house that had lately been turned into a hotel. . . . He entered its magnificent portals, walked up its imposing drive, revolved its revolving doors, and found himself in a large hall with its correct complements of reception-office, automatic cigarette machine, lift, and gigantic porter. And here William realised suddenly that he had formed no plan of action. He did not even know his beloved's name. To demand to see Princess Goldilocks would merely draw down ridicule on him. A glance into a large mirror, moreover, suggested to him that it would have been better to have delayed to make his toilet before presenting himself to anyone in the character of a suitor.

He had set out on his adventure, however, and he did not intend to retreat. . . . While he was cudgelling his

brains for some plan of campaign, the gigantic hall
porter approached him with evident disapproval.

"What do you want, my boy?" he demanded sternly.

It was clear that he did not consider that William's
presence added lustre to the establishment.

An idea flashed into William's ready brain.

"I've come to see someone what's staying here," he
said, meeting the porter's eye unflinchingly.

"Who?" said the porter.

For a moment William was at a loss. He must ask for
some imaginary person. Then, while he waited, he could
think out his plans. But he couldn't think of a name. . . .
Suddenly a word flashed into his mind—the name of the
only river in England that he had got right in the last
geography examination paper.

"Mr. Medway," he said triumphantly.

The hall porter looked over his shoulder at a man
behind a desk.

"Is Mr. Medway in?" he said.

William's mouth dropped open in horror.

"I—I din' mean *that* Mr. Medway," he said hastily,
but neither of them took any notice of him.

"Yes, he came in some time ago," said the man
behind the desk. He craned his neck to look down a
corridor.

"Here he is coming now."

Panic-stricken, William plunged back into the revolving doors. Hardly had he entered them, however, when
he saw the familiar figure of Robert standing just outside
the door talking to a girl. He remembered that when
Robert was in cash he was fond of bringing his inamorata
of the moment to tea at the Cedars Hotel. Hastily he
pushed the doors inward to complete the circle. By this
time, however, a grim-looking man had entered the

hotel hall and the porter was talking to him, unmistakably pointing out William as the boy who had asked to see him. With increasing panic William pushed the door round again. Having done that there seemed nothing for it but to go on pushing it round. One exit would bring him out to confront Robert, who by this time had seen him and was staring at him in indignant amazement, the other would bring him out to confront Mr. Medway, whose expression was as little reassuring. Round and round went William, like a dormouse on its treadwheel, faster and faster as he realised that for the present it was his only means of safety from his enemies.

A small crowd had gathered on either side, watching his revolutions with interest. William saw himself spending the rest of his life in the revolving doors, going round and round till gradually he died of starvation. But someone in authority had arrived, and suddenly the door stopped and refused any longer to be pushed round. Robert, unwilling to be involved in the matter and still more unwilling that his inamorata should learn his relationship to the young ruffian who was causing the disgraceful scene, had hastily remembered that the teas at the Cedar Hotel were very poor and that one could get a far better one at the village inn. William, seeing the coast clear on that side, tried to escape to it, but a powerful hand held his ear and dragged him back into the hotel foyer. There, surrounded by an indignant crowd, he assumed his famous expression of well-meaning imbecility.

"What do you mean by it?" said the man in authority sternly.

"By what?" said William, looking at him unblinkingly.

"By going round and round in that thing."

"WHAT DO YOU MEAN BY GOING ROUND AND ROUND IN THAT
DOOR?" SAID THE MAN STERNLY.

"Oh, that," said William. "I couldn't get out of it. I
mean, we've not got one at home an' I'm not used to
them. It's difficult to make it stop at just the place you
want it to stop at. You push it a bit too far an' then
you've got to go on round again an' every time I pushed
it a bit too far an' had to go round again."

The man in authority had lost interest in the matter. He gave William a glance that consigned him to the lower orders of creation, then turned on his heel and walked away.

"Is this the boy who was asking for me?" said Mr. Medway to the porter.

"Yes, sir," said the porter, giving William the look of one athirst for blood. His dignity was very dear to him, and the scene had detracted from it considerably.

"I suppose you're my nephew, Trevor," said Mr. Medway sternly, and continued at once without waiting for an answer: "You arrive in a disgraceful state of untidiness more than half an hour before the time at which I asked you to call for me, and then you make a fool of yourself and me over that door. A child in its cradle could have managed the thing better."

"I don't think it could," said William, interested in this assertion. "I mean, if it was in its cradle it'd have to get out to push the door, and I don't think it could——"

"Be quiet," said Mr. Medway testily. "And come into the lounge. If there's one thing I detest it's being the centre of a scene."

"Well, you weren't," said William, annoyed at being deprived of whatever limelight there was in the affair. "I don't see how you could have been, considering that it was me that was in the door."

"Be *quiet*!" snapped Mr. Medway again, leading the way into the lounge.

The porter was still directing the bloodthirsty look at William, and William could see for the present no alternative to accepting the doubtful protection that Mr. Medway's avuncular relationship seemed to offer him. He followed him into the lounge, looking round for possible means of escape as he did so. Sitting down by him on a deep settee, Mr. Medway subjected him to a scrutiny that seemed to increase his disapproval.

"It never occurred to you, I suppose," he said coldly, "to brush your hair or wash your face or change your suit before you came to call for me?"

"No," said William quite simply and without resentment.

"I've not seen you for ten years, and I certainly don't seem to have missed much," continued Mr. Medway irascibly. "Well, how are things at home going on? How's your mother?"

"Very well, thank you," said William.

"Very well?" said Mr. Medway in surprise. "She told me in her last letter that she was no better at all."

"Yes, that's what I meant," said William hastily. "Didn't I say that? I meant to say that."

"You seem to me to be half-witted," said Mr. Medway sternly.

"Yes, I am," said William, thankfully accepting this explanation of his mistake. "The doctor says I may get better some day, but just at present I am a bit half-witted."

Mr. Medway glanced at him suspiciously.

"Don't try on any of your funny tricks with me, my lad," he said sharply. "Of course, I know all your family news by letter." His ill-humour seemed to vanish suddenly, and he smiled. "How's Lucy?"

"She's very well in a sort of a way," said William guardedly, trying to be on the safe side. "I mean in one sort of a way she's very well and in another she isn't."

"Your mother said she was quite well when last she wrote," said Mr. Medway.

"Oh, yes," said William hastily. "She is. I meant she *is* quite well. She had a cold last week, that was all I meant. She—she——" William could never resist embroidering a story, and memories of a cold Ethel had caught the week before came to his aid. "She went to a dance and got hot dancing and then went sitting out in the garden with the man she'd been dancing with without putting anything over her evening dress. . . ."

Mr. Medway was gazing at him in bewilderment.

"But—but—Lucy's your mother's new dog, surely?" he said.

William blinked.

"Oh, yes," he said. "Yes, of course. Yes . . . I didn't know you said Lucy. I thought you'd said some other name. I wasn't thinkin' what I was sayin' just for a minute."

"You seem to have a misplaced sense of humour," said Mr. Medway sternly.

"Yes," said William, eagerly accepting this explanation also. "Yes, that's what I've got."

"Well, well, well," said Mr. Medway irritably. "I must say I looked for a little more ordinary intelligence in a nephew of mine. . . . Is Pongo all right?"

William's spirits rose. Pongo, of course, could be nothing but a dog.

"Oh, yes," said William. "He's getting on fine."

"Feeding well?"

"Oh, yes. He has a dog biscuit every morning and some bones in the middle of the day."

"Dog biscuits! . . . *bones!* . . ." exploded Mr. Medway.

"Oh, he has more than that," said William, thinking that Mr. Medway considered the meal inadequate. "He has all the scraps that are left on our plates."

"Dog biscuits . . . scraps on plates . . . is *that* any way to feed a two-year-old child?" thundered Mr. Medway.

William realised that he had made another bad break.

"That was just a joke," he said desperately. "I mean I was thinking of Lucy."

"Your mother said that Lucy lived entirely on raw meat."

"Yes, she does," said the unhappy William. "I mean I was thinking of the dog next door."

The severity of Mr. Medway's countenance had deepened.

"I must say," he said, "that from your mother's account of you I expected a different type of boy. . . . You seem to delight in making untrue statements. You'll be overtaken by Nemesis one of these days."

That seemed a straightforward enough statement.

"No, I won't," said William. "I'm a better runner than she is and I can always beat her. We often have races. She's very well."

"Who is?"

"Nemmysis. . . . The girl what you said was a better runner than me. I had a race with her yesterday, and I won." William thought that it had been clever of him not to specify any particular relationship with the lady. She might, of course, be sister, cousin, or just a friend. . . .

Mr. Medway rose abruptly.

"I won't waste any more time on such rubbish," he said angrily. "You'd better take me to your house now. Wait a minute, though." He again submitted William to the disapproving scrutiny. "I really can't walk through the streets with you in such a state. You'd better come up to my bedroom and tidy yourself."

There seemed nothing for it but to comply. Flight would deliver him into the hands of the gigantic porter who presumably still stood at the front door thirsting for his blood. Reluctantly he went up with Mr. Medway in the lift. It was an automatic lift, the first that William had ever seen. He noticed that Mr. Medway seemed rather nervous in it. Upstairs in a palatial bedroom Mr. Medway turned on the washbasin taps and placed soap and towel in readiness. William carefully scrutinised his face in the looking-glass and took out a grimy handker-chief. "I think it would do with jus' dustin'," he suggested tentatively. But Mr. Medway waved him to the washbasin with a look of stern disdain, and William, with the air of an intrepid hero facing unknown danger, plunged his face into the water, then began to scrub it vigorously. While he was engaged on this operation there came a knock at the door and a boy entered. He was about William's age but startlingly different in appearance—clean and neat, the shine of his hair rivalling the shine of his shoes, dressed in immaculate Etons.

"Who are you?" demanded Mr. Medway.

"I'm Trevor, Uncle," said the apparition.

"Good Lord!" ejaculated Mr. Medway. "Then who's this?"

William had raised his face from the washstand and was watching them through a thick covering of soapsuds.

"That's William Brown, Uncle," said Trevor. "He's a very rough boy, and mother doesn't allow me to speak to him."

The face of Mr. Medway became suffused with an angry purple, and for a moment emotion deprived him of speech. Then he started forward towards William with obviously hostile intent. William dodged neatly and darted out of the room and along the passage. A large open hamper near the lift seemed to offer a good hiding-place. He leapt into it, drawing down the lid, and waited. Soon he heard the voices of Trevor and Mr. Medway.

"Which way did he go?"

"I didn't see, Uncle. Mother doesn't allow me to have anything to do with him. I don't want to say anything unkind about anyone, but he's not the sort of boy mother likes me to know."

WILLIAM WAS WATCHING THEM THROUGH A THICK COVERING OF SOAPSUDS.

"I should think *not!* Well, if you know where he lives, I'll go and see his father. The whole thing's outrageous. I'll speak to the father most strongly, and I hope he'll punish him."

"So do I, Uncle."

"But I must say, my boy, that it's a great relief to find that you're my nephew and not that ruffian."

"I'm sure it is, Uncle."

"Well, well, well," said Mr. Medway, "we won't waste any more time on him. . . . Come along." He opened the lift gate, pressed the 'Ground floor' button

"THAT'S WILLIAM BROWN, UNCLE," SAID TREVOR. "HE'S A VERY ROUGH BOY, AND MOTHER DOESN'T ALLOW ME TO SPEAK TO HIM."

and the lift disappeared. William emerged from his basket. He was deeply interested in the automatic lift. He pressed the button to see what would happen. It so chanced that Mr. Medway and Trevor had just reached the ground floor, but had not yet unfastened the gate. They were wafted up again to the second floor. William heard their ascending exclamations of indignation and surprise in time to take refuge behind the lift.

"There's no one here," said Mr. Medway, looking through the bars as the lift stopped. "How extraordinary!"

He pressed the ground floor button again, and the lift began to descend. This time William, emerging from his hiding-place, was on the alert for the second when the lift should touch the bottom.

Immediately he pressed the button again, and up shot the lift once more still containing Trevor and Mr. Medway. Mr. Medway, to whom it had never occurred to press the button marked "Stop", again peered anxiously out of the bars.

"Still no one here," he said. "I don't understand it at all."

Again he pressed the button and again the lift shot down, only to shoot up again from the ground floor before Mr. Medway had time to open the gate. This happened half a dozen times in quick succession, till Mr. Medway's face, glaring through the bars, had assumed a look of pallid terror, and Trevor was sobbing aloud. Then William, who was himself growing tired of the proceeding, let them open the ground floor gates. . . . He felt that he was amply recompensed for whatever punitive measures his father might take as a result of their report.

He heard the clang of the gates when they reached the door. He heard the sound of Mr. Medway's voice raised in anger and mingling with Trevor's sobs in the hall.

"The thing's completely out of order. Up and down. . . . Of course I pressed the right button. . . . Up and

down a dozen times at least . . . like a monkey on a stick.
. . . The thing's out of order, I tell you. . . . It's a
scandal . . . a disgrace. . . ."

"I feel so sick, Uncle, with going up and down like
that. Lifts always make me sick."

"I tell you we might have been *killed* . . . up and down
and up and down like a mad thing. . . . I've a good mind
to sue you for damages. . . ."

"I'm *going* to be sick, Uncle. . . ."

"Come along, my boy, come along quickly."

The voices died away.

William returned behind the lift again to consider his
position. It was not reassuring. He was marooned on the
second floor of a large hotel, his escape cut off by a
gigantic porter who was presumably still thirsting for his
blood. He was vaguely aware that his interrupted
washing operation had not improved his appearance.
The soap had dried upon his face, and his hair stood up
in a semi-circle of stiff spikes round his brow. He made
an attempt to rub the soap off his face with a pair of
grimy hands, but did not feel optimistic about the result.
He stood looking cautiously about him for some plan to
suggest itself. Suddenly he heard heavy footsteps
approaching. He leapt again into the hamper, drawing
down the lid. He had crouched there in the darkness in a
silence broken only by creaks for some moments, when
suddenly he felt himself swung unceremoniously into the
air. His head was banged sharply against the basket
sides, and it was all he could do not to cry out.

"It's 'eavy, myte," said a gruff voice. "Thought it was
supposed to be empty."

"This 'ere basket-work weighs 'eavier than what
you'd think," said a second voice. "I've often noticed
it."

William, holding his head in both hands to protect it from further contact with the sides of the hamper, heard the sound of a door opening and the first gruff voice saying: "'Ere's the 'amper, Miss. An' proper 'eavy it is, too."

"Nonsense," replied a sharp, feminine voice. "It can't be heavy. There is nothing in it. . . . Well, don't stand dawdling there. Put it down and go."

With a bang, which caught agonisingly a corner of William's head, the men flung down the hamper and departed.

"Cadging for a tip!" muttered the feminine voice indignantly. "Pretending it was heavy! What rubbish! Well, come on . . . we'd better get to work."

"Yes, miss," said a second voice.

There was a quick movement, and the lid of the hamper was thrown back. William, reclining in the basket, his hands to his head, found himself gazing up into two faces. One was evidently that of a maid. The other was as evidently that of Princess Goldilocks. But she did not look as she had looked on the stage. She looked older and less sweet. Much older and much less sweet. In fact every trace of the radiant youth and sweetness that had so charmed William had vanished. At close quarters she looked elderly and irritable. . . . William arose from his nest slowly and with as much dignity as he could muster. He noticed on a sofa a pile of theatrical clothes, which Princess Goldilocks and her maid had evidently been repairing.

"What are you doing in that hamper?" said Princess Goldilocks, fixing an angry gaze upon him. William was silent, returning her in imagination to the brigands and pirates and wild beasts from which he had in imagination so often rescued her.

"I said what were you doing in that hamper?" snapped the lady again.

"I was mendin' it," said William distantly. "I was just passin' and I saw it wanted mendin', so I got in an' mended it an' then those two men came an' carried it away an' nearly broke my head off."

"I don't believe a word of it," said the lady furiously; "show me *where* you've mended the hamper."

"Jus' there," said William waving his hand in a gesture that included not only the hamper but also the entire room. "You naturally can't see where it's mended, because it's mended an' it looks jus' like the rest of it. I'd jus' finished mendin' it when those men came along and nearly broke my head off."

"I don't believe a *word* of it," said the lady again, stamping her foot. "What *business* have you to be mending the thing in any case?"

"I'm employed by the hotel mendin' things," said William unblushingly. "I'm employed by the hotel to go round seein' if anythin' wants mendin' an' mendin' it."

"Stop talking such nonsense!" exploded the lady. "No hotel would employ a dirty ragamuffin like you for anything. You're a thief, that's what you are. Trying to gain entry to my rooms to steal my jewels. . . . What's the matter with your face?"

"It's half washed," explained William. "I mean, I was in the middle of washin' it when something interrupted me an' I had to stop."

"You look a *dreadful* sight. What's your name?"

"Trevor Monkton," said William promptly. "My uncle's staying in the hotel. He's called Mr. Medway. He's a very rich man."

The lady blinked. . . . If the thing had to get into the papers—and she liked everything connected with her to get into the papers—she must be sure of her ground. It wouldn't do to mix the two stunts of laying a small but violent boy thief by the heels and taking part in a practical joke inaugurated by the mischievous and unconventional nephew of a millionaire. . . .

"Anyway," said William. "I can't stay any longer. I'm very busy this afternoon. Good-bye."

He disappeared abruptly. His disappearance seemed to convince Princess Goldilocks of his criminal character. . . .

"Stop him," she screamed to her maid. "Heaven *knows* what he's taken. Quick, quick, quick! Stop him."

They both came running out after him towards the lift. William entered it calmly, closed the gates with slow deliberation, put out his tongue at them through the bars, then pressed the "Ground floor" button and vanished.

Hysterical screams of "Stop thief!" followed him. William emerged from the lift into the hall. The porter advanced to meet him with the air of one about to deal out a long-delayed vengeance. But when he came close to the lift he stiffened and stood listening intently.

"What's that?" he said.

Cries of "Stop thief!" still floated down the lift well.

"Sounds like someone callin' for help," said William with an expression of innocent interest. "It might be a gramophone or some sort of wild beast, of course, but it *sounds* like someone callin' for help."

"Crikey!" said the big porter vulgarly, and pushing William aside he leapt into the lift, pressed a button, and vanished from sight.

William was out of the unguarded door like a flash of lightning. Like a flash of lightning he shot along the road, and down the field path till he reached the neighbourhood of his home. There he paused, drew breath, straightened his collar and tie, stroked back his soaped spikes of hair, assumed his most effective swagger and, congratulating himself on having discovered the illusory nature of love before it was too late, sauntered slowly home to tea.

Chapter 8

Their Good Resolution

"We've gotter decide what good resolutions we're goin' to make this New Year's Day," said Henry.

Henry always took life more seriously than the other Outlaws.

"Yes, they're all goin' on at me about that at home," said Douglas without enthusiasm.

"I think it's silly havin' good resolutions for New Year's Day," said Ginger. "It would be much more sens'ble to have pancakes same as on Shrove Tuesday or bonfires same as on the Fifth of November. I can't think who *thought* of good resolutions. He must have been potty. They aren't any fun for anyone, aren't good resolutions."

"Well, we've gotter choose what we'll have," said Henry. "They've been on at me at home about it all mornin'. They want me to choose tidiness, but I'm jolly well not goin' to. Once you've chosen a thing like that, you get no peace."

"Mine want me to choose punctuality," said Ginger, "but I said I wasn't goin' to make up my mind in a hurry. I mean, once you choose things like punctuality they all start naggin' at you every time you're a bit late ten times worse than they did before."

"Mine wanted me to choose bein' helpful," said William, "an' you know what that'd mean. It'd mean they'd expect me to work for them all the time. Choosin' a resolution like that's the same as sellin' yourself for a slave. Besides, I did choose bein' helpful one New Year's Day, and I did a helpful thing to every one of my family, but they all turned out wrong, an' no one would even believe I meant to be helpful, an' I made up my mind I'd never try to be helpful again."

"The thing we choose doesn't last longer than the day, does it?" asked Ginger anxiously.

"No, it doesn't," said William firmly. "They try to make out it lasts all the year, but it jolly well doesn't. What I say is that, if good res'lutions last all the year, then pancakes an' bonfires an' fireworks ought to, an' they wouldn't let those, so they mustn't 'spect good res'lutions to. No, it's jus' for the day."

"Well, do let's choose which one we'll have," said Henry impatiently.

"My mother wanted me to choose cleanness," said Douglas, "but I think that's the worst of all to choose."

"Yes, I bet it is," said William fervently, "but tidiness an' punctuality are almost as bad. It's simply *askin'* for trouble to choose any of them. I vote we choose somethin' that's *good* all right but not a lot of trouble —like not worshippin' idols or killin' anyone or turnin' Communists or coinin' false money."

The Outlaws considered these alternatives with interest.

"Yes," admitted Ginger, "they're all right in a way. I mean, it wouldn't be any trouble keepin' them an' they couldn't go on at us about them at home, but they're a bit dull. I mean, there's nothing to *do* in them. I'd like to *do* something."

"*Tell* you what!" said William excitedly, "let's rescue someone! That's a *jolly* good resolution."

"Who shall we rescue?" said Ginger.

"Anyone," said William. "There mus' be hundreds of people wantin' rescuin'. Well, you've only to read books to know that. You hardly ever read a book that hasn't got someone imprisoned by villains or held to ransom or something like that. An' I bet in real life," he added, lowering his voice in a sinister fashion, "there's *more*."

"Yes, but how do we find them?" said Ginger, to whom something of William's excitement had already communicated itself.

"We *look* for them," said William. "They won't be easy to find, of course, because nat'rally people that have got people imprisoned keep them jolly well hidden, but, if we set out to look for them, I bet we find them."

Henry and Douglas were slightly less optimistic, but they agreed that it was an excellent idea, and that it completely solved the good resolution problem.

William, his brows drawn into the tense frown that marked his position as commander-in-chief of the band, began to direct his forces.

"It's no good all four of us goin' out together," he said. "They'd see us comin' an' be on their guard. We must split up into twos so that we can creep onto them before they know we're comin'. I votes me and Ginger go together, and Douglas and Henry go together, and I bet me and Ginger 'll find someone to rescue first. . . ."

"Where'll we go, anyway?" demanded Douglas.

"Anywhere," said William sternly. "Use your sense. Go anywhere. Jus' go on till you find someone wantin' rescuin' an' then rescue them. That's what we're goin'

to do, and I bet we needn't go far. People in these books
don't, anyway. They hear screams for help on the first
page, and they've started rescuin' on the second. I bet
once you start lookin' for someone to rescue you find
'em pretty quick. . . . We'll all meet here again after tea
an' tell each other about our rescues. I bet it's a jolly
sight better good resolution than any of the soppy things
they tried to make us choose at home. . . . Come on,
Ginger."

The four set off, Henry and Douglas rather reluctantly. The adventure appealed to them, but they did not
like the thought of undertaking it without William's
leadership. They had an uneasy suspicion that William
and Ginger would perform innumerable feats of rescue,
but that their own search for the kidnapped and oppres-
sed would be a fruitless one.

"The thing to do," William was saying to Ginger as
they went, "is to examine every house we pass *carefully*.
It's no good thinkin' that they're not keepin' prisoners
in their house jus' because they're people that our
fathers and mothers know, and that we've been to tea
with. One thing I've learnt from tales in books is that the
people who seem most all right on the outside are always
the worst really. We'll look in at their windows and listen
very hard to see if we can hear any cries for help."

*   *   *

The afternoon passed quickly. All the houses in the
village—the Vicarage especially, because the Vicar's
position covered him with suspicion in William's eyes
—were subjected to these tests. William and Ginger
crept round each, peeping furtively into all the downstairs windows, but in none of them did they see a bound

victim being forced by torture to sign away his money. They listened intently at every door, but from none issued the muffled cries for help that they hoped to hear. Where trees were conveniently situated, William climbed them in order to look into the upstairs windows, but empty bedrooms were all that met his sternly suspicious gaze. Despite the caution and furtiveness of their approach, however, their visits were not always undiscovered. One old woman, suddenly seeing William's face with his nose flattened whitely against her window-pane, and, thinking with some justification that he was an evil spirit, tried to exorcise him by the simple means of going to the door and flinging a Prayer Book through the darkness in his direction. It was a heavy Prayer Book and caught him sharply on the side of the head. As an exorcism it was wholly successful. . . .

In another garden an old man, finding them creeping through his garden, had pelted their fleeing forms with sods of earth that wrought havoc on their collars and hair. They reached the end of the village without having discovered a single object for their good resolution. Even the Vicar had been discovered merely playing patience in his study.

"Well," said Ginger, slightly discouraged, "what'll we do *now*?"

William's face was set in grim determination.

"We'll go on to Marleigh," he said: "it's only two miles up the hill. I bet we find plenty of 'em *there*."

They walked up the hill to Marleigh in a silence that was broken occasionally by William's saying: "Yes, I bet we find any *amount* of them in Marleigh. I don't expect Henry and Douglas have found any yet, either. . . . We're bound to find some in Marleigh all right."

The first house they came to in Marleigh was a medium-sized house set back a little from the road. William gave his orders to Ginger in sibilant undertones.

"You stand at the gate," he said, "and I'll go up to the window. If I see anyone held prisoner, I'll nod three times."

Ginger stood obediently by the gate, his eyes fixed intently on the figure of his chief as it made its cautious way up the drive, creeping from shrub to shrub. In an unnecessarily circuitous manner it approached the house. Ginger saw its head raised to the window and silhouetted sharply against it. Then suddenly it turned and unmistakably nodded three times.

Forgetting secrecy, Ginger galloped joyfully up the drive, receiving a stern admonition to silence as he approached his chief. Then he stood with William gazing through the window into a large room full of children ranging from infancy to about three years. Some were lying in cots; others played about on the floor in playing-pens. A young woman was with them, dealing out toys and picture-books.

"Kidnapped children," hissed William in explanation of the scene.

"Are you *sure*?" said Ginger, who had formed high hopes of something luridly melodramatic and to whom the scene looked disappointingly peaceful and domestic.

"'Course it is," said William. "What else could it be? It couldn't be one fam'ly. Not *all* those children. They're kidnapped, that's what they are. Someone's holding them to ransom. I shouldn't be surprised if that girl's kidnapped, too, an' they're makin' her look after them. . . ."

The girl turned suddenly towards the window. William and Ginger ducked, then crept round the house to

the front door. It bore a brass label with the word:
"Crèche".

"Look!" said William excitedly. "That's his name.

"KIDNAPPED CHILDREN," HISSED WILLIAM.
"ARE YOU *SURE*?" SAID GINGER.

Kreetch. That proves it. He's a foreigner. Kidnappers
are always foreigners . . . Kreetch. Fancy him having
the cheek to put his name on the house when he's got all
those children held to ransom in it. . . ."

A slight sound within the house sent them running
down the drive to the security of the road.

A YOUNG WOMAN WAS DEALING OUT TOYS.

"Well, are you goin' to rescue them?" said Ginger.

William considered the problem with frowning brows.

"I wish they were grown-ups," he said at last wistfully. "If we rescued them, we'd have to find out who their mothers are and take them back, and as like as not they wouldn't believe they'd been kidnapped, and make it out to be all our fault . . . I'd rather rescue ten grown-ups than one baby any day. I never seem to have any luck with babies. Everything I've ever had to do with babies has ended by getting me into a row, whether it was my fault or not. Their mothers never seem to want to listen to reason. . . . *Tell* you what! We won't axshully rescue them ourselves. We'll jus' tell the police about them, an' then we'll go on an' find someone grown-up to rescue. . . ."

Ginger, who was as unwilling as William to take upon himself the responsibility of a roomful of homeless children, agreed to the suggestion.

"If they were grown-ups," he said, "or if we knew where they lived it would be different. We'd jus' let 'em out an' they'd go to their own homes themselves."

"Yes," agreed William bitterly, "an' *I* know what babies are like. Screamin' an' scratchin' an' pullin' your hair when you're doin' all you can for them. . . . Let's find a policeman quick, so that we can get on with findin' a grown-up who knows where he lives to rescue."

A policeman appeared obligingly round the corner at that moment, and William approached him importantly.

"I say," he said, "there's a man called Kreetch livin' in that house, an' he's got a whole roomful of kidnapped children."

The policeman was young and rather pompous. He frowned down at them in Olympian displeasure.

"You run off," he said, "and don't try to make game of me, or you'll find yourselves at the police station."

They ran off obediently, not stopping till they were well out of sight. Then they began eagerly to discuss the situation.

"He's in league with him," said William. "He's in league with this Kreetch. He'd have put us into prison if

"YOU RUN OFF," SAID THE POLICEMAN, "AND DON'T TRY TO MAKE
GAME OF ME."

we hadn't run off jolly quick. He'd have made up some
tale about finding us robbin' a house to get us put in
prison out of the way, 'cause he knows we've found out
about Kreetch and him. Well, I'm not going to tell any
more policemen. I bet they're *all* in league with Kreetch.

I'm goin' to write to Scotland Yard. I say, it's gettin'
jolly excitin', isn't it?"

"Yes," agreed Ginger heartily, "it jolly well is.
What'll we do now?"

"We'll go on tryin' to find a grown-up to rescue," said
William, "an' I bet we'll soon find one. Well, it stands to
reason we will. If we find a whole roomful of kidnapped
children in the first house we come to, it stands to reason
that we'll jolly soon find a grown-up. . . ."

A thorough investigation of each house of the village
from the outside, however, revealed no suspicious
features, and their spirits began to droop slightly.

"Of course," said William, "it's jolly hard to tell. I
mean, some of the walls look jolly thick, and it would be
jolly hard to hear a cry for help through them. . . . I
didn't like the look of that man that chased us out of his
garden. I thought he'd got a villain's face all right. An'
why should he chase us out of his garden if he'd not got
something to hide? We weren't doing any harm in his
garden. . . . Only lookin' in at the windows. I bet he's
got someone hidden away in his house that he didn't
want us to find, someone that he's tryin' to make sign his
money away. I votes we go back there. We've been right
through the village, haven't we?"

"There's another house round the corner," said
Ginger, "but I think it's to let, so it wouldn't be any
good."

But William's eyes had widened.

"Why, that's just the sort they'd *choose*," he
said excitedly. "They'd *choose* an empty house to keep
them in. I bet there's more kidnapped people kept in
empty houses than anywhere. Come on. Let's go to it
quick."

The empty house was some distance down the road,

and, as they approached it, William's eagerness increased. The blank, uncurtained windows seemed inexpressibly sinister. The very "To Let" sign, affixed tipsily and askew on its board, spoke of lawless happenings. The neglected, overgrown garden seemed full of dark secrets. . . . The gathering dusk deepened its air of mystery.

"I *bet* we find someone here," said William. "Come on. Let's go up to the door and listen to see if we hear voices."

They crept up to the front door and pressed their ears against it. Faint but unmistakable sounds of voices reached them.

"There *is* someone," hissed William. "I bet it's someone keepin' someone prisoner. I can *tell* it is by the sound of the voice. . . ."

Quietly he tried the door. It was unfastened and opened onto a bare, unfurnished hall with a flight of steps running up from the middle of it. They entered cautiously, and stood just inside the door, listening. The voices came from upstairs. They sounded louder now, but still it was impossible to make out actual words.

With a look of grim determination on his face, William sat down on the floor and began to take off his boots. Ginger did the same. Then they crept silently up the stairs in their stockinged feet, holding the boots in their hands. As they reached the top, a door opened somewhere and the voices became louder. Quick as lightning William darted through the nearest doorway, dragging Ginger with him. It was a bathroom. William pushed the door to and looked round for a hiding-place. There was none, so he motioned to Ginger to stand with him against the wall behind the door. They stood there, holding their breath. The voices came nearer. They were

just outside the door now. Suddenly the door was closed
firmly from outside and the key turned in the lock.

"I always keep this door locked," said a man's voice.
"The window catch is broken. . . . You'd think that
burglars would leave an empty house alone but they
don't. We've had empty houses stripped of fittings from
top to bottom in a night. I'll have the window catch
mended, of course. . . . You like the house on the
whole, then?"

"Oh, yes, quite," said a woman's voice vaguely. "It's
rather far from the station for my husband, that's all. We
quite like the house . . . but we don't want to decide in a
hurry. We have several other houses to see."

The voices died away as the agent ushered his client
down the stairs and out of the front door. The sound of
the closing of the front door re-echoed through the
house. Too late William realised his position and began
to beat loudly and unavailingly upon the locked door.

"*Crumbs!*" he said as he relinquished the attempt and
rubbed his bruised knuckles on his coat. "*Now* what're
we goin' to do?"

"What about the window?" said Ginger.

They went over to the window. It opened onto the side
of the house, flat, bare, and sheer to the ground. There
was no obliging scullery roof, no foothold of any sort.
Even the drain-pipe was well out of reach of the window.
The optimism of William and Ginger failed them as they
considered the prospect.

"You couldn't get out *that* way," said William, "not
without killin' yourself, anyway. Let's try knocking on
the door again. There might be someone else in the
house."

They knocked on the door till their knuckles were
sore, then returned to the window. Dusk had become

merged in darkness now, and the sense of adventure that had sustained them so far began to flag.

"It was a long way from the other houses," said Ginger, "with fields all round. S'pose—s'pose we have to stay here all night."

"*That's* not the worst it might be," said William grimly. "S'pose we have to stay here *days* without any food. S'pose no one else comes to look at it, an' it stays empty for years, an' we stay here till we're starved to death. I've read in books of things like that happening. People finding skellytons in houses that no one's been in for years. Jus' skellytons with bits of clothes hangin' on. Prob'ly our families 'll think we've run away to sea or been eaten by wild beasts or something. They'll never think of lookin' for us here, anyway. An' I bet that woman likes one of the other houses better. I bet she never comes here. An' you hear of houses standin' empty for years. . . ."

An expression of horror had overspread Ginger's round and healthy face at the sinister suggestion.

"I say," he gasped, "let's shout for help out of the window. Someone might hear us. Let's shout for help as loud as we can."

"Yes," agreed William, "I votes we'd better try that now."

Abandoning their characters of rescuers of the imprisoned, the two of them hung out of the open window, shouting "Help!" with all the strength of their lungs.

Suddenly from below a voice, muffled by the darkness, floated up to them.

"Hello!"

"We're locked in," shouted William. "Come and let us out."

"All right," said the voice.

*   *   *

Douglas and Henry had spent the afternoon wandering aimlessly about the countryside. Bereft of William's leadership and his all-sustaining faith in the probability of the improbable, they did not know what to do or where to go. They stood at garden gates looking enquiringly at the dwelling-places of peaceful householders till the peaceful householders, annoyed by their scrutiny, came out to ask what they wanted and order them off. It was Douglas who, discouraged by the attitude of the householders, suggested searching barns and outhouses for prisoners.

The search was not altogether successful. They were not challenged by householders, but they were chased by dogs, attacked by ganders, and butted by goats. Henry stumbled into a midden up to his knees in the dusk, and Douglas fell off a haystack from which he was taking observations.

And all the time they had visions of William and Ginger making rescue after thrilling rescue throughout the afternoon.

They did not give up the search till it was so dark that they could not see their way, and it seemed useless to spend any more time peering into barns and outhouses, in which they could not have seen a bound and gagged figure even if one had been there to see. It was when they were nearing the village on their way home that Douglas suddenly stiffened, and stood still.

"Listen!"

Henry listened.

Faint but quite unmistakable cries of "Help!" floated through the darkness.

"It's over there. Across the field," said Douglas.

They made their way across the field in the direction of the cries. As soon as they were near enough Douglas replied: "Hello."

"We're locked in," came the reply; "come and let us out."

So hoarse with shouting was William's voice that Henry and Douglas did not recognise it.

"All right," replied Henry and at once made his way with Douglas round to the front door.

"I bet this is as good as any William will have found," he said excitedly.

The front door was locked, but they found a tiny unfastened window that led to the hall cloak-room and through this they squeezed themselves with some difficulty. Douglas was slightly apprehensive when he found himself in the empty house.

"S'pose it's a trap," he said. "We'd better not rescue them till we've found out a bit more."

Henry, however, was fired by enthusiasm. It was a pleasant change from falling into middens and being butted by goats.

"'Course it's not," he said. "Why should it be? Bags me tell William about it. I bet I can make it sound more excitin' than you. . . . An' we can bring him to show him the house to-morrow to prove it's true. Listen, they're knocking on a door upstairs. Come on. . . ."

"I wonder who it is," said Douglas still more apprehensively and keeping well behind Henry. "If it *is* a trap we shun't have much chance. Was it a man's voice or a woman's? If it was a man's, I vote we go and fetch someone grown up. . . ."

But already Henry was unlocking the bathroom door. . . .

He flung it open and for a few moments the four Outlaws stood staring at each other, paralysed by amazement. Then speech returned to all four simultaneously.

"Crumbs!" they gasped.

*   *   *

They walked slowly homewards. William and Ginger were rather silent. They had tried to make the most of the Crèche episode, but it happened that the omniscient Henry knew the meaning of the word, and that he had, moreover, actually visited the establishment with his mother, who was on the committee. William and Ginger tried to put a good face on this and to pretend that both Henry and his mother—and indeed the whole committee—had been deceived, but their attitude lacked conviction.

"Funny that it was *us* that did a rescue and not you," said Henry for the hundredth time.

"Funny it was *you* we rescued," said Douglas also for the hundredth time.

"Well, we've done *our* good resolution, anyway," said Henry.

"And you've not," said Douglas. "Funny that we've done ours and you've not."

William knew that it would be long before the memory of the afternoon died away and that meantime he must endure frequent references to it with as good a grace as possible.

"Funny to think that p'raps we've saved your lives," said Douglas to whom Ginger had indiscreetly confided their fears. "Funny for you to think for the rest of your lives that if it hadn't been for us you'd be skellytons."

But William had stood as much as he meant to stand

for one day.

"I'm changing my good res'lution," he said firmly. "I'm goin' to make a diff'rent one."

"What are you goin' to make?" said the Outlaws with interest.

"I'm makin' one to go to bed early," said William. "Good night."

Chapter 9

William's Invention

The Outlaws walked dejectedly along the road. Their dejection had been caused by a remark of Henry's.

"This time next week," he had said, "we shall be back at school."

It was a tactless reminder, and its result was to alter completely not only the Outlaws but everything around them. It changed the Outlaws from lords and monarchs of the whole world to slaves and bondsmen. It made the sun shine less brightly, it changed the sky from blue to a dull grey.

"It's awful," said William at last, "the way we spend all our lives goin' to school. It never gives us a chance to do anything great."

"What do you want to do great?" inquired Douglas with interest.

"Lots of things," said William. "I want to be like Napoleon or someone like that, and I never get a chance."

"You couldn't be like Napoleon," objected Ginger, "Napoleon was a soldier, and you can't be a soldier, because there isn't a war on."

"Well, then I want to be great by inventing something."

"What could you invent?" said Ginger.

William considered.

"Everything's been invented," he said at last gloomily. "I could have invented electricity or the telephone or the wireless, but they've all been invented. There's nothing left to invent, or else I'd invent it all right."

"I bet there's lots of things left to invent," said Ginger.

"What is there, then?" challenged William.

"Well, we don't know 'cause they aren't invented," said Ginger. "Why don't you invent some of them if you want to be an inventor?"

"Well, what *is* there to invent?" snapped William. "You tell me what there is to invent."

"You couldn't invent it if I did," said Ginger.

"I could."

"You couldn't."

"I could. You tell me what to invent and I'll invent it. I'll invent anything you say. . . ."

"Well——"

Ginger was obviously at a loss what to suggest.

Suddenly turning a bend in the road they ran into Mrs. Bott, and the Vicar's wife.

"Now, boys, do look where you're going," said Mrs. Bott sharply, and at once continued the conversation they had interrupted. "Talk about *smoke*, it's something chronic! I tell you, anyone who'd invent something that'd stop our library chimney smoking—well, Botty and me wouldn't mind what we paid him."

She passed on, still expatiating on her library chimney.

The Outlaws stood looking after her.

"There," said Ginger to William, "that's what you can invent. Invent something to stop her library chimney smoking."

* * *

Mr. Bott gazed helplessly at his wife, who was sitting in her elaborately furnished drawing-room as if expecting a visitor.

"But I don't understand, my dear," he said, throwing out his arms; "who is she and what's she coming for?"

"She's writing the series of 'Haunted English Country Houses' in the *Woman's Torch*, I told you."

"Yes, but why is she coming here?"

"I asked her to," said Mrs. Bott simply.

"Yes, but *why*?" demanded her bewildered husband.

"Because I wanted her to do the Hall in her series. All the best houses in England have been done in it, Botty, and I did so want ours to be. I thought that if she did do it she might put in that snap of you and me in the rose garden. I think that's ever so sweet. I'd love our home to be in the *Woman's Torch*, Botty, with photos and all."

"Yes, but it *isn't* haunted," protested her husband. "How can it be in a series of Haunted English Country Houses if it isn't haunted? Did you tell her it was haunted?"

"Oh, no, Botty," said his wife. "I'd never tell an untruth. Not a *real* untruth. I—well, I sort of *hinted*, but I didn't tell a real untruth. I'm not going to tell a real untruth when she comes either. I'm only going to—to sort of *hint*. But I do so want to be in that series, Botty, with photos and all."

Mr. Bott groaned and ran his fingers through his hair.

"Well, don't expect me to have anything to do with it," he said.

"No, Botty," said his wife meekly, "I won't."

Still groaning and running his fingers through his hair, Mr. Bott plunged out of the room.

Almost immediately afterwards Miss Manes, the *Woman's Torch* representative, was announced.

She was a tall, thin, angular woman with straight hair that was just too long, and an earnest expression. She sat down in an easy chair, and at once took a little note-book out of her pocket.

"Now, Mrs. Bott," she said briskly, "please tell me *everything*."

"Well," said Mrs. Bott guardedly, "there really isn't *much* to tell. . . ."

"Ah, but there's *something*," said the woman. "I know there is. People are always just a little reluctant to tell me at first—even people who, like you, have actually sent for me. They begin to regret having asked me to come—but, believe me, Mrs. Bott, the world at large has a right to know of the psychic phenomena taking place in your home."

Mrs. Bott, who didn't know what psychic phenomena meant, said: "Yes, indeed," and sighed.

"Have you—have you ever *seen* anything, Mrs. Bott?"

"N-not exactly *seen*," admitted Mrs. Bott mysteriously.

"No? Perhaps your husband has then?"

"N-no," said Mrs. Bott again in the mysterious voice that was being so successful. "No, he hasn't exactly *seen* anything. Oh, Miss Manes, I *do* hope that you'll be able to have that photo of the rose garden in and me and Botty on the terrace. . . ."

"Yes, yes . . ." said Miss Manes rather impatiently, "but to return to the—er—influence. You've seen nothing. Now have the maids ever seen anything?"

"N-no," admitted Mrs. Bott again, "not to say actually *seen*."

"No guests staying in the house have seen anything?"

"Not *seen*," said Mrs. Bott, "not actually *seen* . . .

but, oh, Miss Manes, I do hope that you'll put in a photo of the house from the front drive. It looks a treat from the front drive. Quite ancestral."

"Yes," said Miss Manes again impatiently, "but to return to this—er—influence. You *feel* something around you, I suppose?"

"Yes," said Mrs. Bott, snuggling back into her easy chair so as to assure herself that she spoke the truth.

"You—you hear things?"

"Yes," admitted Mrs. Bott, again assuring herself that she spoke the absolute truth.

Miss Manes leant forward and fixed her piercing eyes on her hostess.

"*What* do you hear?" she said.

"All sorts of things," said Mrs. Bott and added: "I've got a sweet little snap of Botty in shooting things. Could that go in? He's only worn them once because he isn't really any good at shooting, but it came out awfully well except that he's moved his head a little."

"We'll see, we'll see," said Miss Manes, waving aside the snapshot of Botty in shooting things. "Now these sounds you hear . . . what exactly are they?"

"They're—they're just sounds," said Mrs. Bott rather feebly.

"Yes, but what *sort* of sounds?"

Mrs. Bott was silent for some moments then had a flash of inspiration.

"It's so difficult to describe sounds," she said. "I wonder if you'd like a photo of my little Chin Chin for the article. He's got a weak digestion, but he's a sweet little fellow. He'd have won a prize at the Crystal Palace if his tail had been shorter."

"Yes, yes, I'm sure he would," said Miss Manes impatiently, "but this—influence. Can you describe any definite instance in which it's made itself felt?''

Mrs. Bott considered deeply and finally said: "N-no, on the whole I don't think I can."

It was clear that Miss Manes's interest was waning. She was in fact beginning to wonder what on earth the woman had brought her all this way for. This was certainly not the sort of thing she wanted for her series of "Haunted English Country Houses". She was in the act of rising from her chair to take her departure, when she suddenly froze into immobility, her eyes fixed on the doorway behind Mrs. Bott.

"Look!" she said sharply.

Mrs. Bott wheeled round. The doorway was empty.

"What's the matter?" said Mrs. Bott, alarmed by her guest's expression.

"You saw nothing?"

"No."

Miss Manes's manner had completely altered. Her eyes were bright, her cheeks flushed, her whole thin body quivered with eagerness.

"Do tell me more . . . do tell me more . . . you've *never* seen anything?"

"Never."

"Describe the whole house to me. I want a detailed description of it . . . and as much as you know of the people who were here before you."

In the middle of Mrs. Bott's description of the house, Miss Manes's long, thin form froze again; again her eyes gleamed and started; again she pointed with a quivering finger at the door behind Mrs. Bott's head, saying: "*Look!*"

Again Mrs. Bott looked and saw nothing.

"Tell me more . . . tell me more," said Miss Manes excitedly. "Describe to me *exactly* how you feel when you—when you *feel* things."

There was, however, no need for Mrs. Bott to rack her brains. Miss Manes described Mrs. Bott's feelings so well that even Mrs. Bott, completely lacking as she was in what Miss Manes called the "psychic sense", was impressed. In the middle of the description Miss Manes was transfixed yet a third time with starting eyes and pointing finger. Again Mrs. Bott turned round to see only an empty doorway. But now there was no end to the photographs Miss Manes wanted. She was anxious even to print the one of Chin Chin and the one of Botty in shooting costume where his head had moved. She was flatteringly, gratifyingly interested in every detail that Mrs. Bott could give her. She filled pages of her little note-book. When she had finished she closed her note-book and fixed her piercing eyes on Mrs. Bott.

"And now, Mrs. Bott," she said, "I'm going to tell you something that will give you rather a surprise. Prepare yourself for a shock."

Mrs. Bott prepared herself, guiltily suspecting that Miss Manes was going to tell her that she knew the whole thing was a fraud.

"You say that no one's ever seen this thing?"

"Er—yes," admitted Mrs. Bott.

"You've never seen it?"

"Er—no."

"Well"—Miss Manes paused, as one pauses before delivering a bombshell, then brought out her startling news: "I've seen it!"

Mrs. Bott started.

"*You?*"

"Yes . . ."—Miss Manes's voice sank to an impressive whisper—"and more than that, I've—seen—it—three—times."

"No!" gasped Mrs. Bott.

"Yes," said Miss Manes dramatically, "three times it has appeared in that doorway only to vanish as you turned round. It's a blood-curdling sight, Mrs. Bott. No wonder that you have those *terrible* feelings about it though you have never seen it. I confess that at first I was inclined to put your feeling down to imagination. I had even decided not to include your house in my series. But *now*—three times have I seen it standing there—the most unearthly, sinister creature that my eyes have ever met."

"W-w-what's it like?" stammered the terrified Mrs. Bott.

"Black," said Miss Manes impressively, "black from head to foot. Its eyes gleam through the blackness. Quite small, but—but indescribably sinister, Mrs. Bott. The sight of it turns your blood to ice."

"Oh, my!" gasped Mrs. Bott.

The situation was like a nightmare. To find that there was a *real* ghost. . . . She'd never sleep another wink. She wanted the woman to go quickly so that she could find Botty and tell him. "Black", "gleaming eyes", "indescribably sinister". She felt she was going to have hysterics in another minute. But Miss Manes would not go. She was avid for the slightest detail about the house. She was thrilled as she had never been thrilled before. In all the other houses it had been a case of questioning maids, of embellishing unsatisfactory material. Never before had she actually seen the ghost with her own eyes. She insisted on taking away with her every photograph of the Hall that Mrs. Bott possessed. She took with her photographs of Mr. and Mrs. Bott. She took the snap-shot of Chin Chin. She said that she would demand extra space for the article. At last Mrs. Bott got rid of her, then

turned, still aghast and distraught, to find her husband.
She had decided that she couldn't stay in the house
another night. "Black" . . . "gleaming eyes" . . .
"turned your blood to ice". . . . She wanted to have
hysterics, but she wanted to find Botty first. She burst
open the library door. Her husband was not there, but,
standing on the hearthrug in front of the fireplace, was—
the spectre! Black, with gleaming eyes, indescribably
sinister. She opened her mouth to scream, when a well-
known voice came from the horrible figure.

"I'm tryin' to stop your chimney smokin'."

Mrs. Bott approached fearfully. The figure stood in a
heap of soot by the open fireplace. It was covered with
soot, but beneath the soot she could dimly discern the
features of William Brown.

"I'm tryin' to stop your chimney smokin' like what
you said you wanted doin'. I've fixed somethin' up in it
that ought to do it. It's a sort of bellows an' the string
comes out here, an' you pull it and it blows the smoke up
the chimney, an'"—aggrievedly—"I came three times
to ask you to come and look at it, but you'd got a visitor
an' I thought you wouldn't want me disturbin' you——"

"How did you get in?" said Mrs. Bott.

"I got in through the window. I wanted it to be a
s'prise for you. Then, when I'd got it fixed up and
wanted you to see it, you'd got a visitor. Look, I'll show
you how it works. . . ."

But Mrs. Bott was in the full flood of her long-delayed
attack of hysterics.

When she came out, she looked around her again.
William was watching her suspiciously.

"I don't know what you're laughing at," he said
coldly.

"You're *covered* with soot," she said, wiping her

"I'M TRYIN' TO STOP YOUR CHIMNEY SMOKIN' LIKE WHAT YOU SAID
YOU WANTED DOIN'," SAID WILLIAM.

eyes, "and you've *ruined* the hearthrug."

William seemed to realise this for the first time.

"I didn't know such a lot of soot had come down with
me," he said apologetically—"You see, I had to get
right up the chimney to fix up this invention for you,
an'—well, the soot came down with me when I came
down, I suppose."

"I don't know *what* your mother will say."

William examined himself more closely.

"Crumbs!" he said at last, horrified by the results of his examination. Then he looked again at the pile of soot in which he stood, and an expression of yet deeper dismay came over his soot-covered features, as he admitted: "Yes, I am in a bit of a mess."

But Mrs. Bott was smiling. The nightmare of the black spectre with gleaming eyes was over. She could sleep safely in her bed to-night. And the Hall would be a prominent feature in the "Haunted English Country Houses" series. Even the snapshot of Chin Chin would appear.

"Never mind, William," she said, "I know you meant well." She slipped a shilling into his hand and added: "I'll get you as clean as I can, and then I'll come back home with you and explain to your mother, so that she won't be cross."

"An' about this invention," said William. "Next time you have a fire, will you try it an' let me know?"

"Yes," promised Mrs. Bott, reassuringly. "I'll let you know."

Chapter 10

Aunt Arabelle in Charge

The news that Ginger's parents were going abroad for a fortnight was received by Ginger and his friends, the Outlaws, with an exhilaration that they strove in vain to hide.

"We'll have the conservatory for our jungle camp," said Ginger.

"And we'll play Alpine Sports on the front stairs," said William.

"We can get up a bear hunt with the rug from the drawing-room," said Douglas.

"And we can have a *fine* time with those African weapons in your father's dressing-room," said Henry.

Ginger, not wishing to seem too unfilial, added: "I'm sorry they're goin', of course, but it isn't as if they weren't comin' back."

"An', after all, it's only a fortnight," said Henry, "an' we'll put all the things back again so's they'll never know we've had them."

Their exhilaration was slightly damped when they heard that an aunt of Ginger's, who had not seen Ginger since he was a baby, was coming to keep house in his parents' absence.

"If she's like *some* aunts——" said William, speaking

with gloom and bitterness from an exhaustive acquaintance of those relatives.

"She may be all right," said Ginger. "She writes things for papers."

The spirits of the Outlaws rose again. They had met several people who wrote things for papers and had found them refreshingly absent-minded and conveniently blind to their immediate surroundings.

"She'll prob'ly never notice what we're doin'," said William. "If she's like some of 'em she'll watch us doin' Alpine Sports down the front stairs an' never know we're there at all."

"I hope so," said Ginger, "'cause my mother's goin' to give me ten shillings when she comes back, if my aunt says I've been good."

They showed signs of interest and excitement at this news. It was the custom of the Outlaws to have all things in common, especially tips.

"Oh, we'll get that ten shillin's all right," said William confidently. "She'll be so busy writin' soppy tales that she'll be as good as blind an' deaf."

The appearance of Ginger's aunt was certainly reassuring.

She was a small, short-sighted woman with ink-stained fingers and untidy hair. She took her duties in what Ginger considered a very proper spirit.

"I'm a busy woman, dear boy," she said to him, "and I simply can't be disturbed at my work, so you must try not to bother me with *anything*. Just look after yourself and solve your own little problems as best you can. There's no reason why we should trouble each other at all except in case of an absolute *crisis*."

So Ginger looked after himself and solved his own little problems and on the whole solved them very well.

The problems consisted chiefly of how to turn the conservatory into a jungle, how to organise a really good bear hunt with the aid of the drawing-room hearthrug and Ginger's father's treasured assegais, and how to make the staircase into a satisfactory Alpine sports ground.

The last problem was solved by placing mattresses down the length of the staircase. William and Ginger became expert ski-ers, Henry was content to climb up and down with the aid of Ginger's father's alpenstock and Douglas's speciality was rolling down it inside an empty linen basket.

William, who had written a play that had been acted by his followers, and a serial story that had been published in a newspaper of his own editorship, and who therefore considered himself a full-fledged member of the profession of letters, took a great interest in Aunt Arabelle's activities.

"You tell her I'll help her if she gets stuck in a tale," he said to Ginger, "tell her I'm jolly good at writin' tales. Well, I've never read a better tale than that one I wrote called 'The Bloody Hand'."

"I have," said Ginger.

"I bet you haven't," said William. "It's the best tale anyone's ever written. I wrote it, so I ought to *know*."

It occurred to William that it would be a kind action if he added a few helpful touches to Aunt Arabelle's manuscript while she was out taking her daily "constitutional", as a pleasant surprise for her on her return.

"I bet I can write about ghosts moanin' an' rattlin' chains as well as anyone," he said.

"P'raps she doesn't write that sort of tale," objected Ginger.

"Then I can write about dead bodies and findin' who killed 'em."

"There's other sorts of tales than that," said Ginger.

"No, there isn't," said William firmly, "not that anyone ever wants to read, anyway."

But an exhaustive search of Aunt Arabelle's desk revealed no stories of any sort—only a typewritten sheet headed: "Answers to Correspondents." The first was: "I am sorry, dear, that he has not spoken yet. But just go on being your own sweet self, and I am sure he will soon."

"What's that mean?" said Ginger with a mystified frown.

"It's someone who's got a dumb child an' is tryin' to cure it," explained William in all good faith. "What's the next?"

"I understand so well, Pansy dear," read on Douglas, "the anguish and turmoil that lives beneath the brave front you turn to the world. Probably he feels the same. Couldn't you find some mutual friend to introduce you? Then I am sure all will be well."

"What's that mean?" said Ginger, looking still more mystified.

William himself looked puzzled for a minute. Finally enlightenment seemed to come.

"It's someone what's got stomach-ache an' she's tellin' 'em to get to know a doctor what's got stomach-ache too, so's he'll know how to cure her. It's a jolly good idea. I often wish our doctor had stomach-ache when I have it. I bet he'd try'n' find a nicer medicine if he'd gotter take it himself."

The next day William boldly tackled Aunt Arabelle on her literary work, kindly offering to give his help if she wished to turn her art to fiction.

"I've written some jolly good tales," he said, "an' I wouldn't mind helpin' you a bit."

"I'VE WRITTEN SOME JOLLY GOOD TALES," SAID WILLIAM, "AN' I
WOULDN'T MIND HELPIN' YOU A BIT."

"No, thank you, dear boy," said Aunt Arabelle.
"You see, I don't go in for fiction."

"It's much more interestin' than writin' to people
about dumbness an' stomach-ache," said William.

"But I don't do that, dear. I help them in their little
troubles of the heart."

"Well, I think diseases are all dull," said William,
"whether they're heart or stomach-ache or anything

else. What do you write them for?"

"For a little paper called *Woman's Sphere*. I don't only do the Answers to Correspondents, of course. I sometimes do interviews. But," she sighed, "it's difficult to get *really* interesting people to be interviewed for the *Woman's Sphere*. It's only a Twopenny, you see."

But William, whose literary experience was confined to fiction, had lost interest in her work, though, liking always to be up to date, he made a mental note that Answers to Correspondents should form a part of the next paper he edited.

"I don't think much of her," he said to Ginger, "writing rot like that about hearts an' stomachs an' dumbness an' things."

"She's better than any of your aunts, anyway," said Ginger, feeling that the honour of his family must be defended.

"Oh, is she?" said William, accepting the challenge. "All right, you tell me one of my aunts she's better than."

"The one that asked why they only used one goal post at a time when she came to see the rugger match."

"Oh, is she? Well, let me tell you she's not. I'd sooner have her than one that writes rot about hearts an' stomachs an' dumbness."

"*An'* the one that told your father that it was wrong to take life in any form and that green fly had as much right to existence as he had."

The argument degenerated from this point into a discussion on aunts in general and finally took the form of a rivalry for oddness in aunts, from which Ginger emerged triumphant with Aunt Arabelle.

The pursuits, however, that had been so exciting during the first few days of her visit soon began to pall.

The conservatory had its limitations as a jungle, the hunt with assegais proved interesting only to a certain point (assegais were unwieldy weapons and prone to bite the hand that fed them), and, though Alpine Sports on the staircase retained their charm the longest, their delights too were exhausted before the end of the first week.

Then the Outlaws began to look round for fresh interests. They were torn between a desire to return to the woods and fields that were the usual scenes of their activities, and a feeling that to leave house and garden of Ginger's home in the present circumstances was to waste a golden opportunity that might never occur again.

For Aunt Arabelle, shut in the library, writing her Answers to Correspondents and articles on How to Beautify the Home or Feed the Husband or Renovate the Wardrobe on a Small Income, remained blind and deaf to all their doings, and the domestic staff of Ginger's home had long since washed their hands of him.

"Let's think of something *really* exciting to do," said William.

It was Ginger who thought of it.

"Let's have a sea fight in the conservatory with paper boats an' sticks to guide 'em," he said. "We can turn on the tap enough to have the floor jus' under water, an' the floor's made of tiles so it won't do it any harm, an' we won't have enough to go up the step into the hall."

The idea was adopted eagerly by the Outlaws, and they set to work at once making fleets of paper boats. Then they flooded the conservatory. They found that as the "sea" trickled out beneath the door into the garden it was necessary to replenish it at frequent intervals. It was Ginger's idea to leave the tap on, "Just enough to keep a decent sea," and in the excitement of the ensuing naval conflict they did not notice that the tap had been left on too full and that the water was rising above the step into the hall.

Aunt Arabelle, a far-away smile on her lips (she had just written a very beautiful little article on the Art of the Love Letter), stepped from the study to the hall and was brought down to earth abruptly by finding herself standing in a large pool of water. It struck cold and clammy through the moccasins that she always wore when she was working. It swirled around her ankles. Aunt Arabelle clutched her skirts about her in terror, and, without stopping to consider the particular element that was threatening her, shouted: "Fire!" The cook rushed out from the kitchen with the fire extinguisher, and, as she had completely lost her head and as Aunt Arabelle was still shouting: "Fire", proceeded to drench Aunt Arabelle with its contents.

The Outlaws heard the commotion and hastily turned off the tap. But it was too late. Aunt Arabelle had been roughly shaken out of the hazy vagueness in which she usually lived. Some of the contents of the fire extinguisher had gone into her mouth and the taste was not pleasant. The apple-green smock in which she always worked was ruined. In short, the "absolute crisis" had arrived in which she had decreed that she and Ginger should trouble each other.

"I can't *possibly* tell your mother you've been good now," she said to Ginger.

The Outlaws, who, in the intervals of devising the new games, had planned the spending of Ginger's good conduct money to the last farthing—and had even spent some of it on credit at the local sweet shop—were aghast. They used their utmost powers of persuasion on Aunt Arabelle but in vain. "I can't possibly," said Aunt

Arabelle simply. "I'd be telling an untruth if I said that Ginger had been good, and I couldn't *possibly* tell an untruth."

It was a point of view from which they found it impossible to shake her. Gloom descended upon them. Even the house had lost its charms. They walked down into the village, carefully avoiding the local sweet shop. And in the village they met Anthony Martin. They did not know that he was Anthony Martin, of course. They saw a little boy of about six, picturesquely attired, wearing a complacent expression, and hair that was just too long. He was a stranger to the locality.

"Who are you?" said William.

"Don't you know?" said the little boy with a self-conscious smile. "I'm Anthony Martin."

William's face remained blank. The little boy seemed disappointed by their reception of the information. "Don't you know Anthony Martin?" he said.

"No. Never heard of him," said Ginger.

A shade of contempt came into the little boy's face.

"Good heavens!" he said, "whatever sort of books do you read?"

"Pirates an' Red Indian stories," said William.

The boy looked pained and disgusted.

"Good *heavens*!" he said again. "I shouldn't have thought there was *anyone*—— Haven't you read any of the Anthony Martin books?"

"No," said William, unimpressed. "Did you write 'em? I've written books myself."

"No, my mother writes them, but they're about me. Poems and stories. All about me. Nearly half a million copies have been sold, and they've been translated into fourteen different languages. I've had my photograph in literally hundreds of papers. *Good* papers, I mean. Not rubbish. They're *literary* stories and poems, you know. Really cultured people buy them for their children. There were several Anthony Martin parties in London last year. *Hundreds* of children came. Just to see me. Have you *really* never heard of me?"

William had never met anyone like this before, and he was for the time being too much taken aback to do himself justice. He merely gasped: "No . . . never."

"You can't know much about *books*, then," went on the child scornfully, "and your people can't either, or they'd have bought them for you. They're *the* children's classic nowadays. I have *hundreds* of letters from people who've read them. People I've never met. They send me presents at Christmas, too. And——"

"Why have you come here?" said William, stemming the flood.

"My mother's come for a rest," said Anthony Martin; "she's been overworking. And people have been rushing us so. I've got *sick* of Anthony Martin parties. But it seems unkind to disappoint people, and they do so love to see me. We're going to spend a very quiet fortnight down here. I'm not going to give any interviews. Except perhaps one. The editor of *The Helicon* wants to send someone down, and I've half promised to be photographed on her knee. Of course, I don't *quite* know whether I shall yet. Well, I must go home to lunch now. Tell your people you've seen me. They'll be interested. I simply can't understand your never having heard of me. Good morning."

The Outlaws stood open-mouthed and watched Anthony Martin's small, dapper figure as it strolled nonchalantly away.

Then they turned gloomily homeward. The incident had increased their depression. They found Aunt

Arabelle dried and changed and in a state of great
excitement.

"My dears!" she said, "you'll never *guess* who's
come to stay in the village. Anthony Martin!"

"We've seen him," said William dejectedly.

"But, my dears, aren't you *thrilled*?"

"No," said William.

"You know his *sweet* things, don't you?"

"No," said William.

"Oh, I must read some to you. I've got them nearly all
here. I never go anywhere without them."

The dejection of the Outlaws deepened still more.

"You've actually *seen* him?" went on Aunt Arabelle
eagerly.

"Yes."

"Oh, my dears, I *must* see him. I wonder—No, I
suppose it would be *impossible*——"

"What?" said Ginger.

"I have written several times officially, and I've had
no answer. Of course the *Woman's Sphere* isn't *quite*
. . . I mean, they can't be *expected* . . . but he does give
interviews quite a lot."

"Oh, yes," said Ginger, "he said he was doing that.
Being photographed on someone's knee."

"Oh, *lucky* someone!" said Aunt Arabelle ecstatically. "Did he say what paper?"

"Sounded like a pelican," said William.

"*The Helicon*," said Aunt Arabelle humbly. "Ah,
yes, of course. . . ." And she sighed deeply, wistfully.

William looked at her, and the ghost of the lost ten
shillings glimmered faintly on his mental horizon.

"Do you want him to interview you very much?" he
said.

"The other way round, dear boy. I want him to grant

me an interview with *him*. More than anything else in the world."

"Do you know where he's staying?" said William.

"I heard that they'd taken Honeysuckle Cottage," said Aunt Arabelle. "I must try to get a *peep* at him anyway."

When Anthony Martin strolled out into the garden of Honeysuckle Cottage after tea, he found the four Outlaws standing in a row at the gate. Anthony Martin was accustomed to people's hanging about to catch a glimpse of him and took it as his right, but the Outlaws' ignorance had piqued his vanity. He strolled up to them slowly.

"I simply can't make out how you've never come across those books," he said. "They're *everywhere*. All the bookshops are full of them. There was my photograph in nearly all the bookshops last Christmas. And there was an Anthony Martin Christmas card. Why, I could go out to tea every day of the year if I wanted to."

"Look here," said William, making himself the spokesman, "will you give an interview to Ginger's aunt? It's a *very* important paper."

"We'll let you play Red Indians with us if you will," said Ginger.

"We'll show you the best place for fishing," said Henry.

"We'll take you to our secret place in the woods," said Douglas.

"Good *heavens*!" said Anthony Martin contemptuously. "That sort of thing doesn't appeal to me in the *least*. . . . What is the paper?"

"It's called *The Woman Spear*," said Ginger.

"Never heard of it. What sort of thing does it go in for?"

"Dumbness and stomach-ache and heart disease and things like that," said William.

"I've never given an interview to a medical paper before," said Anthony Martin importantly. "Look here—our agent's coming over to see us to-morrow. I'll ask him. He knows all about these papers. Come here this time to-morrow, and I'll let you know."

So high had the hopes of the Outlaws risen in the interval that by the time they assembled at the gate of Honeysuckle Cottage the next evening they had borrowed sixpence from Victor Jameson on the strength of the ten shillings and made new and revised arrange- ments for the expenditure of the rest.

The small and picturesque figure swaggered down to them through the dusk.

"Well?" said Ginger eagerly.

"It's a jolly good paper," said William, "it's got better stuff on dumbness and stomach-ache and heart disease than any other paper going."

"We'll give you sixpence of it," said Henry, referring to the ten shillings and forgetting that Anthony Martin didn't know about it.

"We'll show you a tit's nest," said Douglas.

Anthony Martin dismissed the whole subject with a wave of his hand.

"It's absolutely off," he said. "Our agent says that it's a piffling paper and that I mustn't on *any* account give an interview to it. It hasn't even any circulation to speak of."

"It does speak of circulation," said William, pugna- ciously, "it's included in heart disease."

"You don't know what you're talking about," said Anthony Martin loftily. "Our agent says it isn't a medical paper at all. It's a twopenny-halfpenny rag."

"It wouldn't do you any harm jus' to give her an interview," pleaded Ginger.

"My dear boy, it would," said Anthony Martin. "It would cheapen our market, and that's the last thing we want to do. . . . Anyway, my mother said you could come to tea to-morrow if you liked."

"Thanks awfully," said William with a fairly good imitation of politeness.

"I want to show you some of our Press cuttings," said Anthony Martin.

It was clear that he felt a true missionary zeal to convert them to his cult.

"Don't bring your aunt," he warned them, "because

"HOW *SWEET* OF HIM TO ASK YOU HERE," SAID ANTHONY
MARTIN'S MOTHER. "HUNDREDS OF PEOPLE WOULD GIVE
ANYTHING FOR THE PRIVILEGE."

I shan't see her. And it's no use your telling her things I say because she can't use them without our permission."

The next day the Outlaws presented themselves, clean and tidy, at Honeysuckle Cottage. They were first of all taken to Anthony Martin's mother, who lay on a sofa in the front room with the blinds down, garbed in an elaborate rest gown, her head swathed in a sort of turban. She raised a limp hand in protest as they entered.

"Oh tip-toe, please, boys. Every sound goes through my head. I'm always like this between the visits of my

THE OUTLAWS POLITELY TRIED TO LOOK IMPRESSED BY THIS
INFORMATION.

creative genius. Prostrated. No one knows what I suffer. . . ." The limp hand raised a pair of lorgnettes from among the folds of the elaborate rest gown, and she surveyed the four in silence for several moments. The result of her inspection seemed to deepen her gloom. "How *sweet* of him to ask you," was her final comment. "I hope you realise that hundreds of people would give almost *anything* for the privilege. I hope you will remember this afternoon all your lives. . . ." The limp hand dismissed them with an airy wave, then went to her suffering head as the Outlaws clumped their way out.

Upstairs, Anthony Martin had a suite all to himself, consisting of a small sitting-room, a small drawing-room, and a small bedroom. This self-contained kingdom was presided over by a crushed-looking creature in a cap and apron whom Anthony Martin addressed as "Nurse," and treated with the hauteur of an Oriental despot.

"I want you to hear my latest record first," he said to his guests. "Mother's having records made of the Anthony Martin poems recited by me. She's going to give four very select Anthony Martin parties when we get back to London and she's having the records made for that. They're not being issued to the public yet. This is 'Homework'. It's a very popular one. Every verse ends with 'Anthony Martin is doing his sums'."

He put on the record, and the Outlaws listened to it in a dejected silence.

"I'm making another one to-morrow," went on Anthony Martin when it was finished. "A man's coming in from Hadley with the thing, and I recite into it, and then they make the record from the impression. I'm going to do 'Walking in the Puddles' to-morrow. Mother likes me to be quite alone with her when I recite them for records. Anyone else in the room disturbs the atmosphere.''

He took down a large album and gave it to William. "You can look at the Press cuttings, and I'll take the others into my bedroom and show them the toys that come in the stories. You can go downstairs and fetch up the tea now, Nurse.''

William was left alone in the little sitting-room with the album of Press cuttings. He turned the pages over idly.

Suddenly the door opened, and a man entered carrying a kind of gramophone.

"As the front door was open," he said, "I came straight up with this 'ere. It wasn't wanted till tomorrow, but as I was over with something for the Vicarage I thought I'd leave it."

He looked at William in surprise.

"You aren't the young gent, are you?"

"No," said William hastily, "he's in his bedroom."

"Well, never mind botherin' him," said the man; "jus' tell 'im I've brought it. I'll explain 'ow it works in case they've forgotten. It's all ready for takin' the impression an' all they have to do is pull out this 'ere and that lets the sound through to the wax. Then take out the finished impression—'ere—and bring it down to us an' we'll fix it up.'' He looked round the room and finally set down the instrument behind a small settee. "That's nice an' out of the way till they want it to-morrow, isn't it?"

Then he creaked downstairs and out of the open front door leaving William gloomily turning over the pages of the album. The crushed-looking nurse brought up tea and the six of them took their places round the table. Anthony Martin alone sustained the conversation. He had still a lot to tell his new friends, still a lot to show them. He had a letter signed by a Royal Personage. He had a present sent to him by the wife of a Cabinet Minister. He had a photograph of himself taken with an eminent literary Celebrity. The crushed-looking nurse interrupted this monologue to say:

"Now drink up your milk, Master Anthony."

"Shan't," returned the world-famous infant.

"You know the doctor told your mother you'd got to drink a glass of milk every tea-time."

"You shut up," said the winsome child.

"Your mother said I wasn't to let you get up from tea till you'd had it," said the nurse.

Anthony Martin turned on her with a torrent of invective which showed that, as far as mastery over words and their fitness for the occasion was concerned, he had inherited much of his mother's literary talent.

During it William remembered that he had forgotten to tell them about the man with the gramophone. Then a sudden light seemed to shine from his face. He slipped from the room and returned in a few minutes, leaving the door ajar, ostentatiously flourishing his handkerchief and muttering: "Sorry, left it in there." Anthony Martin proceeded undisturbed with his "scene", his voice upraised shrilly:

"Shan't drink it up. . . . All right, you try to make me, you old hag. I'll throw it in your nasty old face. I'll kick your nasty old shins. I'll stamp on your nasty old toes. You leave me alone, I tell you, you old cat, you! I'll tell my mother. Do you think I'm going to do what you tell me now I'm famous all over the world? I——"

It went on for five or ten minutes. William sat listening with a smile on his face that puzzled the others. It ended by Anthony Martin's not drinking his milk and the depressed nurse's feebly threatening to tell his mother

"ALL RIGHT, YOU TRY TO MAKE ME DRINK IT," SHOUTED ANTHONY
MARTIN, "AND I'LL THROW IT IN YOUR NASTY OLD FACE."

when she felt better.

After tea William asked if he might still go on reading
the Press cuttings and if Ginger might look at them with
him as he was sure that Ginger would enjoy them.
Anthony Martin also was sure that Ginger would enjoy
them. "I'll leave you to read them here," he said, "and
I'll finish showing the other two the things in my

bedroom, and then they can read the cuttings and I'll show you the things upstairs."

The other Outlaws were still more puzzled by William's attitude. They felt that he was pandering to this atrocious child without getting them anywhere. They followed his lead as ever, though in a reluctant hang-dog fashion that was small tribute to Anthony Martin's much paragraphed "charm".

Douglas and Henry followed him gloomily into the little bedroom that partook of the nature of an Anthony Martin museum (Anthony Martin's mother took the stage properties with them even on short visits), leaving Ginger and William sitting side by side on the little settee, their heads bent over the album of Press cuttings. As soon as the door had closed on them, William sprang up, dived behind the settee and emerged with something that he held beneath his coat.

"When he comes down tell him I don't feel well and I've gone home," he said, and slipped from the room, leaving Ginger mystified but cheered, for it was evident that William's fertile brain had evolved a plan.

The man at the gramophone shop down in Hadley received him and his precious burden without suspicion.

"Oh, yes," he said, "tell them I'll have it ready first thing to-morrow. You'll call for it? Very good. An honour for the neighbourhood to have the little gentleman here, isn't it?" William agreed without enthusiasm and departed.

He was at the gramophone shop early the next morning. He looked rather anxious and his posture as he entered the shop suggested the posture of one prepared for instant flight. But evidently nothing had happened in the meantime to give him away. The gramophone man was depressed but not suspicious.

"I think it's a mistake," he said, as he handed the record over to William. "It's quite out of his usual line and personally I don't think it'll be popular. It's not the sort of thing the public cares for."

William seized his parcel and escaped. At the end of the street he met the crushed-looking nurse. She recognised him and stopped.

"Where's the gramophone shop?" she said.

William, still poised for flight, pointed it out to her.

"They sent the thing up," she complained, "a day before we asked for it an' without leavin' no word an' without the proper thing in. We've only jus' come across it behind the settee. An' there's no telephone in the house so I've got to trapes down here. Would you like to come back with me and carry it up?"

"I'm frightfully sorry," said William, "but I'm very busy this morning."

He just caught the 'bus from Hadley. There wasn't another one for half an hour. That gave him half an hour's start. Aunt Arabelle had gone out for the morning constitutional (she called it "communing with Nature") that gave her the necessary inspiration for her day's work. The Outlaws were waiting for him at Ginger's gate and accompanied him at a run to Honeysuckle Cottage. Anthony Martin was strolling aimlessly and sulkily about the garden.

"Hallo," he said; then to William: "Are you better?"

"Yes, thanks," said William.

"I expect you aren't used to such a good tea as you got yesterday," said Anthony Martin and added morbidly: "I'm sick of the country. There's nothing to do in it. It's all very well for writing poems about, but it's rotten to stay in. Mother made up a ripping one last night called 'Staying in the Country'. Every verse ends 'Anthony

Martin is milking a cow.' She's prostrated again to-day, of course."

"Will you come over to Ginger's house?" said William. "We've got something to show you there."

The disgust on Anthony Martin's face deepened.

"It's unlikely *you'd* have anything I'd want to see," he said. "It's your aunt wants to see me, an' I'm jolly well not going to let her."

"No, she's out," said Ginger, "an' it's something you'll be jolly interested in."

"Is it about ME?" said Anthony Martin.

"Yes," said Ginger.

Anthony Martin shrugged petulantly.

"I'm always being shown things in the papers about myself that I ought to have seen first," he said, "the Press cutting agencies are so abominably slack." He threw a bored glance round the garden. "Well, I may as well come as stay here, I suppose, as long as your aunt isn't there."

It was a relief to have secured him before the crushed-looking nurse arrived back with her sensational news.

Anthony Martin accompanied them to Ginger's house, giving them as they went his frank views on the country and the people who lived in it. They received his views in silence.

"Well, what is it?" he said as he entered the house.

"It's a gramophone record," said William.

"Something of mine?"

"Yes."

"My dear fellow, it's not recited by me, because none of them are issued yet. A good many of my things *are* done on records, I know, but not recited by me, and that makes all the difference. Fancy bringing me all this way just for that!"

"It's one you've not heard," said Ginger.

"I bet it isn't. I've heard them all."

"All right. We'll put it on and you can see."

He followed them into the morning-room, where a gramophone stood on a table by the window. In silence William put a record on. There came a grating sound, then a shrill voice tempestuously upraised:

"Shan't drink it up. All right, you *try* to make me, you old hag. I'll throw it in your nasty old face. I'll kick your nasty old shins. I'll stamp on your nasty old toes. You leave me alone, I tell you, you old cat, you! I'll tell my mother. D'you think I'm going to do what you tell me now I'm famous all over the world. . . ."

There was, of course, a lot more in the same strain. Though not the sweet, flutelike voice of the record "Homework", it was unmistakably Anthony Martin's voice. Anthony Martin's aplomb dropped from him. He turned a dull, beet red. His eyes protruded with anger and horror. His mouth hung open.

He made a sudden spring towards the gramophone, but Ginger and Henry caught him and held him in an iron grip while Douglas took off the record, and William put it in a cupboard, locked it and pocketed the key.

"Now what are you going to do?" said William.

The result was a continuation of the record with some picturesque additions.

"It's no use going on like that," said William sternly. "We've got it, and everyone 'll know it's you all right even if they've never heard you go on like that."

"It's illegal," screamed Anthony Martin. "I'll go to the police about it. It's stealing."

"All right, go to the police," said William. "I'll hide it where neither the police nor anyone else can find it. And I'll take jolly good care that a lot of people hear it.

Ginger's aunt's having a party here this afternoon, and they'll hear it first thing. I bet that in a week everyone 'll know about it."

Anthony Martin burst into angry sobs. He stamped and kicked and bit and scratched, but Ginger and Henry continued to hold him in the iron grip.

"Now, listen to us," said William at last. "This is the only record, and we'll give it to you so that you can break it up or throw it away on one condition."

"What's that?" said Anthony Martin checking his sobs to listen.

"That you give Ginger's aunt an interview for her paper and have your photograph taken sitting on her knee same as you were going to for the other."

There was a long silence during which Anthony Martin wrestled with his professional pride. Finally he gulped, spluttered and said: "All right, you beasts. Give it to me."

"When you've given my aunt the interview," said Ginger.

When Ginger's aunt returned, Ginger met her on the doorstep.

"He's here," he said, "and he's going to give you an interview for your paper. And he'll have his photograph taken on your knee. He's rung up the photographer in Hadley to do it, and he'll be here any time now."

All the rest of that day Aunt Arabelle had to keep pinching herself to make sure that she was awake.

"My dears, it's too *wonderful* to be true. So *sweet*, isn't he? Such a *lesson* to all you boys. The things he said in the interview brought tears to my eyes. I only wish you boys loved Beauty as that little child does. It's a wonderful interview. The editress will simply die of joy when she gets it."

William fixed her with a stony gaze.

"We took a jolly lot of trouble getting him to give it to you."

"I'm sure you did, dear boys," said Aunt Arabelle, "and I'm *so* grateful."

"That tap that Ginger left on by mistake——"

There was a long silence during which William and Aunt Arabelle looked at each other, and the connection between the tap and the interview dawned gradually upon Aunt Arabelle's simple mind. Her eyes slid away from William's.

"Well, of course," she said, "when one comes to think of it, no actual *harm* was done. In fact, *really* it was no more than—than just washing out the floor of the conservatory and hall. No, Ginger dear, on thinking the matter over, I see nothing in that episode to justify me in making any complaints to your parents."

Aunt Arabelle stayed for the night of Ginger's parents' return. Ginger's parents were inordinately, as Ginger considered, full of their travels and described them at what Ginger thought undue length. Even Aunt Arabelle grew restive. Finally Ginger's mother noticed the restiveness and said kindly:

"And have you any news, dear?"

With sparkling eyes and flushed cheeks Aunt Arabelle poured out her news in a turgid stream.

"Anthony Martin, you know . . . *the* Anthony Martin . . . yes, *here* . . . a *whole* half-hour's interview . . . and the editress was so pleased that she paid me double my usual terms, and she's going to give me all the important interviews now, and she's raised my rate of payment for all my work."

"How splendid," said Ginger's mother. "And has Ginger been good?"

The eyes of Ginger and Aunt Arabelle met in a glance of complete understanding.

"*Perfectly* good," said Aunt Arabelle. "*Quite* a help, in fact."

"I'm so glad," said Ginger's mother.

"You said ten shillings," Ginger reminded her casually.

She took a ten shilling note out of her purse and handed it to him.

"And now, Ginger dear," she went on, "I want to tell you about some more of the wonderful cathedrals we've seen."

But Ginger had already slipped out to join the Outlaws, who were waiting for him at the garden gate.

Chapter 11

A Little Affair of Rivalry

When Robert refused the secretaryship of the local football club which William knew he had wanted for years, William realised that some new and powerful attraction must have come into Robert's life. It was not the new car, for Robert had had the smart little sports coupé for more than a month now, and, though still very proud of it, he was beginning to be able to take part in a conversation without bringing it within two minutes to cars in general and his car in particular.

During the early days of his car ownership he had acquired an almost sinister mastery of the art of bringing every conversation round to cars. The League of Nations, Epstein's sculpture, the theory of relativity, the situation in the Far East—nothing baffled him. Whatever the circle of which Robert formed a part began to talk about, in two minutes they were talking about Robert's car. But either he was losing his skill in introducing this topic or his friends were acquiring counterbalancing skill in avoiding it. Whichever was the case, Robert's car was now far less in conversational evidence than it had been a month ago. Besides, the secretaryship of the local club would bring Robert's car further into the limelight and give more opportunities

for its use. No, it was not his new car that had made
Robert refuse the long-coveted secretaryship. So William, whose interest in his nineteen-year-old brother's
concerns was unceasing and who knew far more about
them than that brother ever realised, set himself to find
out the reason. He had not far to seek. In fact the first
trail he followed led straight to it. Robert was
notoriously susceptible to feminine charms. Though
susceptible, however, he was no philanderer, for in each
fresh charmer who dawned upon his horizon he always
saw his one and only true soul mate. A long succession of
disappointments had in no way disillusioned him, and he
still gave to each inamorata in turn a devotion that he
looked upon as lifelong.

The first thing William did was to inquire casually of
the cook whether any new inhabitants had lately come to
the neighbourhood. William's store of knowledge of
human nature was creditably large considering his
youth, and he had long since learnt that local news
circulates most swiftly and surely through kitchen channels. The cook informed him that a new family had lately
come to The Elms in Marleigh, a village about two miles
away.

"But no boys," she added sternly, "so you needn't
think to find any more young devils like yourself to play
with there, Master William. Only one young lady, I've
heard, and a nasty little dog that snaps like it was the
fiend hisself. So the postman says, anyhow. *And* you'd
better not go playing tricks in their garden either, 'cause
the master, he's that garden proud you'd hardly believe.
The fuss he makes over his drive—well, the butcher's
man says he takes up every blade of grass before you can
see it, and rakes the gravel hisself every day. He told the
baker's man not to bring his cart into the drive at all

'cause of the mess its wheels made on his gravel. There's no one in that house in *your* line, Master William, so you'll only waste your trouble hangin' about it.''

But William paid an unofficial visit to the house and did not consider his trouble wasted. He saw all the protagonists of Cook's story—an elderly man with a red, choleric-looking face and bushy, white eyebrows, laboriously raking over the gravel of the drive . . . a golden-haired girl with saucer-like eyes, a very pink and white complexion, and a tiny pursed mouth . . . a small Pom that growled and muttered to itself as it walked beside its mistress.

And he saw Robert, Robert driving his new car very, very slowly past the gate of The Elms and blushing a violent crimson as the girl and the Pom emerged. Though the girl pretended not to see him, it was obvious that she was fully aware of his presence and its implication. She called out "Good-bye, father dear," in a voice of silvery sweetness that was evidently intended more for Robert's ear than for the gravel raker's, who indeed paid no attention to it. She gave a prettily ringing laugh as she threw a small stick for the Pom to run after. The Pom, rightly resenting this attempt to use him as a dummy for the display of her charms, ignored the stick and replied to the ringing laugh by a cynical growl. At the gate she stood still and looked up and down the road as if uncertain which way to go, giving Robert, who had stopped the car and was gazing at her soulfully, every opportunity of noting and admiring the saucer eyes and tiny mouth. Then, still affecting not to notice the smart sports car and its languishing occupant, she set off down the road, singing gaily to herself in the sweetly musical voice, the Pom growling an accompaniment at her heels. Then a third person appeared upon the scene: Jameson

Jameson. Jameson Jameson was a contemporary of
Robert's who from childhood had been, as is the manner
of contemporaries, alternately friend, foe, and rival. On
this occasion he was undoubtedly rival. He came slowly
down the road, blushing hotly as he met the radiant
vision, then stood gazing after it with an expression on
his face suggestive of acute indigestion, which William
had learnt to recognise as portraying undying devotion.
The vision apparently failed to see him, but it called
again to the Pom in the musical voice, looked down for a
moment to display the sweeping lashes, looked up to
display the saucer eyes, then proceeded daintily on its
high-heeled shoes. When it had vanished from sight
round the corner of the road, Jameson heaved a deep
sigh and turned to face Robert, who sat in his gleaming
sports car also gazing soulfully in the wake of the vision.
Their eyes met and between them there passed a slow,
challenging glance in which each of them declared his
intention of fighting the other to the death for the favour
of the beloved. Then Robert started up his sports car
with a flourish as if to impress upon his rival the
advantage that it gave him and started off with a very
noisy gear change that he hoped Jameson did not hear.
Jameson smiled a nasty smile in order to show Robert
that he had heard the bad gear change and watched the
car disappear in the distance with an expression of
haughty contempt that plainly showed his consciousness
of the advantage that it gave to his rival.

William had been an interested spectator of these
proceedings through the hedge. Not for nothing had he
been Robert's brother for eleven years. The situation
was quite clear to him, and a feeling of family partisan-
ship made him eager to help Robert by every means in
his power.

When he reached home he found Robert being interviewed by an official of the local football club.

"I hoped you'd have reconsidered your decision," he was saying.

"I'm so sorry," replied Robert, "I'm afraid I really can't take it on. I—I really haven't the time."

"I'd had an idea," said the official, "that you were rather keen on getting the secretaryship."

"I was," said Robert, "till—I mean"—he stopped, embarrassed—"I mean, I really haven't the time, I'm afraid. I—I'"—his embarrassment increased—"well, I really haven't the time."

The official gazed at him, puzzled and unconvinced.

"I mean," went on Robert hoarsely, "I'm needed at home. My—my mother hasn't been well lately."

At this moment Mrs. Brown entered the room.

"I'm sorry to hear that you've not been well, Mrs. Brown," said the official solicitously.

Mrs. Brown, who looked as usual extremely healthy, stared at him in surprise. Robert's face turned a dull purple.

"I—I thought you'd not been looking very well lately, mother," he said hastily. "I was telling Mr. Bryant so."

Mrs. Brown looked still more puzzled.

"But I'm *perfectly* well, dear," she said. "How very peculiar of you to tell Mr. Bryant that."

"Of course what I meant was," said Robert to the guest with a sort of desperate abandonment as of one who has plunged so deeply into the morass that any attempts at extrication must be useless, "I mean, I didn't exactly *mean* that my mother wasn't well; what I *meant* was——" he paused and gave a hollow laugh.

His mother's open-mouthed gaze of surprise and the

official's solicitous, almost nervous, expression disconcerted him.

"What I meant to say was," continued Robert wildly, "that I may not be going on playing football for very much longer. I mean, there comes a time in every man's life when he must stop playing football. I mean, there are other things in life. I mean, one must think of the younger generation coming on. I always dislike to think of older men sticking to posts and going on filling up the football clubs when there are younger generations coming on. I mean, there comes a time when a man has to think of settling down and—and so on. . . . ."

He glanced round desperately, took out his handkerchief to mop his brow, and ended with a burst of inspiration: "Why not ask Jameson Jameson?"

The secretary rose, still watching Robert with a solicitous, nervous gaze.

"Yes, I will. As a matter of fact I know he's keen on it—only I wanted to ask you first."

He took his leave hastily, murmuring to Mrs. Brown at the door: "Keep him as quiet as possible. I think he's got a touch of fever."

"Do you feel quite well, dear?" said Mrs. Brown, returning to her son and placing her hand on his forehead. Robert shook it off impatiently.

"Yes, mother," he said, "of course I feel well."

"I thought you wanted to be secretary of the football club."

Robert assumed an expression of virtue almost worthy of William.

"Yes, mother dear, for some reasons I'd like it very much, but I'd rather think of Jameson having it."

"How unselfish of you, dear," said Mrs. Brown, deeply touched.

Robert had spoken no less than the truth. He did like to think of Jameson having the secretaryship. He liked to think of Jameson being so busy with the duties of the secretaryship that he had no time to hang round the gate of The Elms at Marleigh watching for the vision to appear.

That evening, however, William met Victor Jameson in the village. William and Victor also were contemporaries and, like their elder brothers, had been friends, foes, and rivals, alternately from babyhood.

"They've asked my brother to be secretary of the football club," called Victor triumphantly.

"They've asked mine, too," retorted William.

"Mine's too busy to take on a thing like that," added Victor with an inflection of superiority in his voice.

"So's mine," returned William.

"Mine's gettin' to be friends with some new people at Marleigh," said Victor.

"So's mine," retorted William, "and I bet mine'll get to be friends with her first."

Rivalry was thus declared between them, but for many days the affair remained at a standstill, though the vision, on emerging from her gate, never failed to find the two blushing sentinels awaiting her appearance. Neither of them possessed the courage to accost her or the ingenuity to make her acquaintance in any other way. Jameson, stung by the advantage that Robert's smart little sports car undoubtedly gave him, had bought a new pair of shoes in order to counterbalance it as far as possible. They were in their way as impressive as Robert's car, being composed of very yellow leather freely inlaid with white, and drew the gaze of every passer-by as irresistibly as if they had been a magnet. Rather to their owner's embarrassment, the sight of them sent the Pom into paroxysms of fury, so that he could never pass them without snarling and baring his teeth ferociously. Robert, watching from his car, was at first delighted by the animosity roused in the Pom by Jameson's new shoes, but his delight was short lived, for undoubtedly this animosity between the Pom and the shoes could easily lead to a closer acquaintance between the respective owners, and Robert soon noticed that Jameson, evidently also realising the possibilities of the situation, had begun to make defiant and challenging passes with his feet whenever the Pom appeared. On the morning when the vision called off her pet from a murderous attack upon the shoes and threw a smiling glance of apology at Jameson before she went on her way, William, watching through the hedge as usual, decided that the time for action had arrived. Somehow or other Robert and the girl must become officially acquainted. The prestige of the family was at stake. Never must Victor be allowed to boast that his brother in a pair of new shoes had triumphed over William's brother in a brand-new car. He decided to survey the enemy's forces before he fixed upon any definite plan of action. With this object in view he crept up to the house under cover of the bushes, avoiding the freshly raked and weeded drive, and crouched behind a laurel bush that separated the front door from the bay window of the drawing-room.

Hardly had he taken up his position than to his amazement he saw Robert walk boldly to the front door and ring the bell. William, frozen to immobility behind his laurel, watched and listened with breathless interest.

"Excuse me," said Robert, removing his hat with a flourish, as a trim housemaid appeared, "but does Mr. Rigby live here?"

William gasped with amazement. Strange that Robert, paying this first and momentous call, had not troubled even to learn the real name of the beloved.

"No," said the maid, "no . . . it's Mr. Moston that lives here."

Robert assumed a rather overdone expression of surprise and bewilderment.

"Really . . . well, that's strange. I had a note from a Mr. Rigby asking me to call and see him, and I'm sure he gave this address." He made a pretence of searching in his pockets, then continued: "No, I don't seem to have it with me. You're *sure* Mr. Rigby doesn't live here?"

"Quite, sir."

"Perhaps he lives next door?"

"I don't think so, sir. I don't think he lives anywhere in the road, sir, but I'll find out."

The housemaid vanished and almost immediately the vision appeared in her place. She smiled bewitchingly at Robert. It was clear that she saw through the ruse, but approved it.

"Good afternoon," she said. "What name was it you said you wanted?"

"Mr. Riley," stammered Robert, blushing crimson.

"Oh, not Rigby?" said the vision sweetly. "The maid said Rigby."

"No," said Robert, stammering and blushing still more. "At least . . . at least he used to be called Rigby. Then he came into some money on condition he changed his name to Riley. So that he often gets called both."

"Yes, I see," said the vision. "Is that your car at the gate?"

"Yes," said Robert carelessly, but swelling visibly with pride; "yes, that's just a little car of mine."

"It's awfully smart," said the vision, "it's just the sort

WILLIAM WATCHED THE PAIR WITH BREATHLESS
INTEREST.

"I THINK YOURS IS THE SWEETEST NAME I'VE EVER HEARD,"
ROBERT WAS SAYING.

of car I like."

"Would you—could you——" plunged Robert daringly, clutching at his throat in the stress of his emotion.

But the vision cut him short.

"Well, we must try and find out where this friend of yours lives first. What did you say his name was?"

"Filby," said Robert, trying to collect his scattered wits.

"I suppose he had some more money left him then?" said the vision innocently; "I mean, after he'd had some money left him to change his name from Rigby to Riley, then he had some more money left him to change it to Filby?"

"Er—yes," agreed Robert hastily, "yes, that's what happened."

"Well, father's out, but I know he's got a directory somewhere—so come in and let's see if we can find it."

Crimson-faced with joy and victory, Robert followed the vision into the house.

William did not dare to emerge from his hiding-place till Robert had come out again and the coast was clear.

He amused himself meantime by catching spiders on the laurel bush and organising races between them on the window-sill. Robert did not emerge for half an hour, and when he appeared it was evident that very little of that half-hour had been wasted.

"I think it's the sweetest name I've ever heard," he was saying fervently as he stood on the top step with the vision "Emmeline".

"Most people seem to like it," said the vision modestly. "Do you think it suits me?"

"Terribly," said Robert fervently. "I mean, it—it absolutely *is* you—if you know what I mean. It's the most beautiful name I've ever heard. It—it—well, it absolutely *is* the most beautiful name I've ever heard."

"Yes," said the vision after a slight pause during which Robert's eloquence sought in vain for further gems of rhetoric, "well . . . next Wednesday, isn't it?"

"Yes . . . after lunch."

"You'll be here in good time, won't you, because I hate hanging round."

"I'll be here with the dawn if you like," said Robert ecstatically.

"No, I'd hate you with the dawn," said the vision; "two o'clock will be early enough. Oh—and don't bring the car up the drive, will you? Father's so *terribly* particular about the drive. He can't bear even a wheel mark on it. . . ."

"Righto," said Robert, secretly relieved at not being expected as yet to manipulate the hair-pin bend from the road into the drive. He then departed, turning round at the gate to remove his hat with a courtly flourish. The vision retired, and William, after waiting till the deafening sound of Robert's gear changing had died away in the distance, emerged, spidery and dusty, from his laurelled retreat and crept furtively down through the bushes to the road. He was pleased to see Victor just outside the village. He assumed his most rollicking swagger as he greeted him and said carelessly:

"Did you see Robert comin' out of The Elms jus' now?"

"No, I didn't," retorted Victor incredulously.

"Well, he did do," said William; "he's been in the house talkin' to her all afternoon. He—he's one of her oldest friends now. He knows her name an' everything. I bet he'll be goin' there to tea every day now."

"I don't believe you," said Victor still incredulously.

"All right," said William, "you go there to-morrow

at two o'clock, an' you'll see them startin' out for a
drive. Bring your brother to watch them, too," he added
derisively.

Victor stared at him. He knew when William was
bluffing, and William was certainly not bluffing now.

"There's a spider on your nose," he remarked coldly.

"I know there is," retorted William, rising to the
occasion. "I've trained it to be on my nose."

Whereupon he proceeded on his triumphant way and
did not stop to brush off the spider till he was well out of
sight of Victor.

The next afternoon at two o'clock William went
across the fields to Marleigh to watch affairs as usual
from his unofficial spy post in the hedge. He was
gratified to see Victor stationed a few yards from him
also intent on watching the situation from the safety of
the field. Jameson, wearing the new shoes, patrolled the
road. Robert drew up at the gate in the two-seater. The
vision tripped daintily down the drive, greeted Robert
with a cordiality that was obviously intended to intrigue
the watching Jameson, got into the car by Robert, and
set off with him to the accompaniment of a deafening
crash from his gears. The figure of Jameson followed
them desolately down the road. Even his shoes looked
crestfallen. William turned exultantly to Victor.

"Yah!" he said, "I *told* you so!"

Victor, wasting no time in futile recrimination, closed
with his rival, and a spirited battle took place that,
though indecisive, afforded satisfaction to both sides.

William, of course, was aware that Jameson would
spare no pains after this to gain acquaintance with the
vision and that Victor would help him by every means in
his power. And the next day it turned out that Victor had
found the Pom wandering at the other end of the village,

and had taken it to Jameson, who had restored it to its owner, who had been prettily grateful and had not only asked him to tea but arranged to go out for a walk with him the next day.

William noticed that Victor was going about with his hand bandaged and gathered that the kidnapping of the Pom for the purposes of its restoration had been in its way a fairly heroic action. Between the rivals honours seemed to be easy. Robert's car was an asset that had an irritating and incalculable way of turning suddenly into a liability. There was one painful afternoon when Robert tinkered with it for an hour in an unsuccessful attempt to make it go, finally walked four miles home with an exasperated Emmeline, and was later informed in the presence of Emmeline by the mechanic whom he had sent to the "breakdown", that the engine was in perfect order but the petrol tank was empty.

The fair Emmeline, however, needed both her cavaliers. She liked to play them off one against the other. She talked freely also of yet a third, "my cousin Charlie, who I'm practically engaged to."

Robert, however, was not worried by this. He had had wide experience of damsels of Emmeline's age and, as he said to his mother, "they always talk about someone else they're practically engaged to just to make you feel mad."

Robert's jealousy was centred not on the absent cousin Charlie, but on the ever-present Jameson.

Early in the next week it happened that Robert had arranged to take Emmeline for a drive at half-past two. He arrived at the gate before two, partly in order to prove his devotion and partly in order that he might have time to think out some plan of campaign that would destroy for ever Jameson's chances of winning

Emmeline. Jameson's wits, however, had already been at work, and the smart little sports car in which Robert sat deep in his meditation bore behind it the legend, startlingly visible in green chalk: "The man inside this car is a fool."

Passers-by read the legend, paused to peer grinning for a minute at the unconscious Robert, then, still grinning, passed on their way. So lost was Robert in the problem of how to eliminate Jameson from the lists, that at first he did not notice the grinning faces that appeared and disappeared at frequent intervals. When they began to obtrude themselves upon his notice he took their interest to be a tribute to his beloved car, and, mistaking their derisive grins for smiles of wistful admiration and envy, he assumed an expression of superior detachment befitting the possessor of the marvel. But, as the final mists of his meditation cleared away, he realised that the car was surrounded by a crowd of small boys whose jeering could not possibly be mistaken for wistful admiration and envy.

He leapt indignantly from his seat, scattered and pursued them, then returned to the car and his meditation. But there was a faint uneasiness in his mind. He considered his car to be as fine a car as ran the roads, but even he, proud possessor and ardent admirer of it as he was, realised that it was not unique enough to justify the attention that it seemed to be attracting. Several hundred replicas of it, in fact, passed along that very road every week. And—his uneasiness increased. On closer inspection the smiles were most certainly not smiles of wistful admiration and envy. They were derisive, mocking. . . .

Again and again Robert had to leap from his seat to scatter crowds of jeering little boys. Furtively he rubbed his face with his handkerchief in case it was a smut on his nose that was causing the amusement. Furtively he felt his tie to be sure that he had not forgotten to put it on. He smoothed down his hair. The passers-by continued to show the same disconcerting interest in him. His bewilderment increased. He took out his watch. It was nearly three o'clock, and still Emmeline had not appeared. He glanced up at the window of The Elms, and at one of them he saw the face of Emmeline distorted by some strange emotion. For Emmeline from her bedroom window could read the legend and see the amusement caused by it among the passers-by, and she felt as infuriated and humiliated as if she had been sitting there in Robert's place. Robert, mistaking her expression for one of acute physical pain, leapt from his seat and ran up to the front door knocking loudly.

To the housemaid who opened the door he gasped:

"Your mistress is ill! Go to her, quickly!"

But Emmeline was coming downstairs. Her cheeks were flushed, her eyes blazed.

"Do you think I'd go out with you now," she stormed, "after making a fool of yourself and me like that? I'll never speak to you or have anything to do with you again."

And the bewildered Robert found himself on the doorstep with the front door slammed in his face. He turned away with his hand to his head.

"She's gone mad or I have," he said with deep conviction to the laurel bush that had lately sheltered William.

Then he saw a little crowd at the back of his car, intent, as it seemed to him, on the theft of his spare tyre.

He sprang to its rescue, scattering the crowd—and came face to face with the announcement: "The man in

"DO YOU THINK I'D GO OUT WITH YOU NOW?" EMMELINE STORMED,
"AFTER MAKING A FOOL OF YOURSELF AND ME LIKE THAT?"

this car is a fool". He rubbed it out furiously, watched by
a grinning circle, and crimson-faced sprang into the car
again, intent only upon vengeance.

It never occurred to him to impute the crime to
anyone but William.

There were generally a few outstanding scores between Robert and William, and, as Robert's eight years' seniority gave him an undoubted physical advantage, William would frequently have recourse to such measures as this in order to equalise matters. He drove home quickly, narrowly escaping a collision at the cross roads, and executed immediate vengeance upon the protesting William.

"All right," said William furiously at the end, "now I've *finished* helping you. I've done all I could for you, and now I've *finished* helping you."

"Yes, a lot of help you've been," stormed Robert. "You've just ruined my whole life, as usual, that's what you've done. She'll never look at me again after this."

"No, she jolly well won't," said William. "I'll see she doesn't. You'll be jolly sorry about this. I never wrote that on your car but I jolly well wish I had done, and I'll do something a jolly sight worse now after this, so there!"

Robert emitted a hollow laugh.

"You couldn't," he said. "When a man's life's ruined, it's ruined. Nothing worse can happen to him."

"Oh, can't it," said William darkly, "well, you jolly well wait and see."

He set off across the fields and by chance met Victor.

"I've stopped helpin' Robert," announced William. "Your brother can marry her any day you like now, for all I care."

He thought it best to make it quite clear to Victor that he had withdrawn from competition with him so that Victor should not triumph over him when Jameson won the vision.

"He can't, for all I care," retorted Jameson bitterly. "I'm goin' to do all I can to stop him, anyway."

It was an odd coincidence that that morning the Jamesons' housemaid had absentmindedly cleaned Jameson's new shoes with brown boot polish instead of the special preparation he had provided, with the result that the white inlays that had been Jameson's pride and joy were now stained a uniform and rather dingy brown. When accused by Jameson, the housemaid, whose guiding principle in life was never to admit herself in the wrong in any circumstance whatsoever, denied having touched the shoes, and so Jameson, knowing that Victor had several scores against him, and, moreover, possessed an uncanny knowledge of how best to wipe them out, attacked him both verbally and physically and left him vowing vengeance.

William and Victor confided in each other these cruel examples of the injustice of Fate in general and elder brothers in particular.

"Well, I'm jolly well goin' to do all I can now to stop her havin' anythin' else to do with him," said Victor firmly.

"S'm I, Robert," said William, "an' I bet I do it first."

"I bet you don't. I bet I do it first."

Rivalry was again declared between them.

"But it's not really fair," said Victor, "'cause she never *will* have anythin' more to do with Robert anyway, an' Jameson's all right with her."

But they soon discovered that Jameson was not all right with her. As they reached their vantage point in the hedge, Emmeline and the Pom were emerging from the gate, and Jameson, who had obviously been hanging about in the hope of this happening, stepped forward to greet her, trying to compensate for the eclipsed glory of his shoes by a sweeping flourish of his hat. But the Pom, goaded to a fury by the sight of his old enemies, the white and yellow shoes, appearing in this new and sinister disguise, sprang at Jameson's right foot with a savage snarl. Jameson, reacting automatically to this attack, dealt the Pom a kick that lifted it clear of the road and deposited it, still snarling savagely, several yards away. Emmeline snatched up her pet, her eyes flashing angrily.

"You beast!" she said to Jameson, "you hateful beast! You bully! How *dare* you ill-treat a poor dumb animal like this! I'll never speak to you again."

With that she turned on her heel and left him, tenderly caressing the poor dumb animal, whose snarls and yelps rose deafeningly to the heavens.

Jameson watched her till the front door, shut with an indignant slam, hid her from his sight, then walked disconsolately away.

"There, you see!" said Victor. "We needn't bother. She'll never speak to either of them again."

But there had suddenly appeared at the end of the road the figure of Robert, his face entirely concealed by an enormous armful of flowers.

He passed the disconsolate figure of Jameson without apparent recognition and left it gazing after him in amazement. Then, shedding its disconsolateness, it hastened quickly away.

The animated bunch of flowers that was Robert approached the house, knocked at the front door, and was admitted.

"Crumbs!" said William, impressed despite himself at this proof of the dauntlessness of mankind.

"Look!" said Victor excitedly.

For the figure of Jameson could be seen hurrying along the road, weighed down by an enormous box of chocolates.

"Gosh!" ejaculated Victor impressed in his turn, "he must have run all the way an' back buyin' it."

Jameson also approached the house, knocked at the front door, and was admitted.

The two watchers in the hedge continued to watch.

"She's not turnin' 'em out," said William in a tone of acute disappointment, when five minutes had elapsed. He had had pleasurable visions of the figures of Robert and Jameson fleeing down the drive before Emmeline's wrath.

"Women are jolly funny," replied Victor; "you never know what they're goin' to do. I've often noticed it."

Robert and Jameson suddenly emerged from the house with Emmeline between them. Emmeline was smiling pleasantly. All was forgiveness and serenity. She stood at the gate to see her guests off.

"You'll be here at half-past two to-morrow, then," she said to Robert, "and we'll have a nice little run." Then to Jameson, "And you'll look in later: won't you?"

Then, giving her sweetest smile to each of them, she returned to the house. The suitors bowed to each other stiffly and set off in opposite directions.

"Crumbs!" said Victor in a tone of disgust, "it's all as bad as ever it was."

"Well, we wanted it to be, didn't we?" said William. "How can we pay them out if it isn't? Now we're startin' fair, an' I bet I make it so's she won't speak to Robert before you make it so's she won't speak to Jameson."

"I bet you don't, then. I bet I do it first."

"All right. . . . Look!"

The elderly and irascible-looking gentleman who was Emmeline's father was now walking up the drive, examining the footmarks of Robert and Jameson with expressions of anger and disgust.

He disappeared into the house, then reappeared carrying a rake and accompanied by Emmeline to whom he indignantly pointed out the marks that marred the virgin smoothness of his gravel. Emmeline's plaintive voice reached them: "I can't help them having big feet, father dear. . . ."

Muttering angrily to himself, the man began to rake over the almost imperceptible marks. William watched thoughtfully. . . .

"Well, I'm goin' home now," said Victor, "an' I bet I've nearly got a plan now."

"So 've I," said William.

That evening William looked thoughtfully at Robert for a moment, then said:

"You can't turn your car in at gates yet, can you, Robert?"

"Of course I can," said Robert haughtily. "Why?"

"Oh, nothing . . . only you always seem to leave it outside gates instead of taking it in."

"Nonsense!" said Robert. "I can *easily* drive it inside any gate."

"Can you?" said William with a maddening smile of incredulity.

"'Course I can," snapped Robert. "I can take my car *anywhere*. I can turn in at *any* gate, I tell you."

William repeated the smile and left him.

In the afternoon Robert drew up as usual in the road outside the gate of The Elms and went in to call for Emmeline. Soon he reappeared with Emmeline, walked down the drive with her, and handed her into the car with his most courtly gesture.

Then he walked round the car as he always did now to make sure that its surface was not marked by any slighting reference to the man inside it, got in with Emmeline, and drove off.

He could not know, of course, that while he was inside The Elms William had tied a pot of red paint, into which he had bored a small hole, to the axle of the car. As the car went on its way, a thin, red line followed it along the road.

"What are people staring at us for?" said Emmeline suspiciously.

"They often do stare at this car," said Robert modestly. "It's a nice little car. You don't see many little cars like this on the road."

"It's not that sort of stare," said Emmeline peevishly, "and you see quite a lot of cars like this on the road. It's only a mass production car and quite a cheap one at that."

Robert winced at this rude shattering of the mists of glamour through which he liked to see his beloved car.

"That may be true in a *way*," he admitted distantly, "but, after all, it's the driving, not the actual car, that people notice, and—well"—modestly—"people do like to watch a neat bit of driving. I've often noticed it."

"They won't want to watch you, then," retorted Emmeline; "you've nearly banged into at least three other cars since we started out . . . and why does it make that awful noise every now and then?"

"That's the gear changing," said Robert coldly; "the noise is unavoidable."

"All cars don't do it."

"The best makes do," said Robert, still more coldly. "It's—well, it's quite unavoidable in the best makes."

"Well, I'm sure it's that awful noise that makes people stare at us so."

People certainly were staring—some amused, some

mystified, some suspicious, all interested. Emmeline's peevishness increased. She was a connoisseur in glances of interest, and these were not the particular sort of glances of interest that she was accustomed to provoke.

"Do I look funny in any way?" she said severely to Robert.

"No," said Robert glancing at her, "you look all right."

She tossed her head.

"'All right,'" she echoed, "that's a nice way to put it! Well, I think it's the way you're driving that makes people stare so. You go all over the road and keep on making that awful noise. . . ."

Interest in the progress of the car continued all along its route, and relations between its occupants had become very strained by the time it returned to The Elms. At the gate of The Elms stood William, wearing the smile of derision that he had assumed that morning when he questioned Robert's ability to drive his car through a gateway. Robert had been stung and goaded by his companion's reflection on his driving throughout the afternoon. That smile on William's face was the last straw. With a flourish he turned the car into the gateway of The Elms.

"I'll rake over any marks it makes myself," he said as he drew up triumphantly at the front door.

Then he helped his companion out of the car and followed her into the house. It so happened that neither of them looked back at the thin, red line that marked its track up the otherwise spotless drive.

William stood at the gate watching. His smile of derision had changed to a smile of quiet enjoyment. The scene was laid for the *dénouement* of the drama.

He walked slowly down the road and soon met Victor.

Victor, too, was wearing a smile of quiet enjoyment.

"I bet I've won," he greeted William, "I bet you anything I've won."

"What've you done?" said William.

"He's bought a new hat to come an' see her in," said Victor, "an' I've put glue all along the inside so's it won't come off once he's got it on. I bet that'll do for *him*."

"Well, come an' see what I've done," said William.

To his joy the figure of the owner of The Elms could be seen coming along the road from the station. It had adjusted its pince-nez and was examining with interest the zig-zag line of paint that showed startlingly red along the country road.

He called to the village policeman who was practising circus tricks on his bicycle in a neighbouring lane.

"What's all this?" he said.

"I've no idea, sir," said the policeman, surreptitiously brushing the dust from his clothes. He had fallen from his bicycle several times in trying to dispense with the handle bars.

William joined them.

"I saw a man carrying a dead body that he'd murdered down this road——" he began.

But he had not really hoped to be believed. The policeman, who knew him well, only made a threatening gesture and said: "Get along with you."

The policeman then subjected the red line to the tests of touch and taste and said: "Seems to be paint, sir."

They followed the red line down the road, accompanied by William. When the owner of The Elms saw it turn into his gate, his eyes protruded and his cheeks flamed a red crimson.

At the door stood Robert's car in a miniature lake of

red paint. The man rushed into the house and soon emerged, holding a bewildered Robert by the collar.

"*Ruined* it, you have, with your monkey tricks," he was shouting. "I've a good mind to wring your neck. I *will* wring your neck if ever I catch you round here again."

"I assure you, sir——" gasped Robert. "I've no idea——"

"I could sue you for damages for this. I *will* sue you for damages for this. Off with you, you puppy, and take your tin lizzie with you."

With that he hurled Robert down the short flight of steps from the front door. Robert, still bewildered, picked himself up, got into his car, and drove hastily away. The red line followed him down the drive, and Emmeline's father, his hands raised to heaven, cursed him loudly and in such picturesque terms that the policeman coughed deprecatingly and said: "Come, come, sir."

William was leaping about exultantly in the road: "I've done it. I've done it first," he said, "I said I would."

Victor looked crestfallen.

"Well . . . let's just wait till Jameson comes along," said Victor. "I want to see him try to take his hat off."

They waited. After a few moments the figure of a young naval officer came along the road from the station, turned in at the gate of The Elms, and was admitted to the house.

"Who's *he*?" muttered William, feeling indignant at the appearance of a new actor on the scenes at this juncture.

"Look!" said William.

The owner of The Elms now emerged carrying a pail

in one hand and a kneeling-mat in the other. His face was still crimson with rage. He muttered fiercely to himself as he knelt down and began carefully to put the paint-covered gravel into the pail.

"Let's go," said William, "nothin' more's goin' to happen."

But something more was going to happen. At that moment there came the sound of grinding gears and Robert appeared in his car. He looked pale and nervous and drove very carefully. On the seat beside him was a box of chocolates and a bunch of flowers. He stopped the car at the end of the road and, dismounting, crept cautiously towards the gate of The Elms to see if the coast was clear. At the same moment Jameson appeared from the other direction wearing the new hat that he had bought in order to compensate for the dimmed glory of his shoes.

Just as they met at the gate, there emerged from the front door of The Elms Emmeline and the naval officer. They walked arm in arm and beamed resplendently. They passed the muttering figure that was still at work upon the gravel and came down to the gate where Robert and Jameson stood gaping side by side. She smiled upon them radiantly and flourished a white hand upon which sparkled a diamond ring.

"My cousin Charlie that I'm engaged to," she introduced her escort before she passed on.

Jameson was too much overcome to try to remove his hat, much to the disappointment of Victor who was anxious to see the results of his handiwork.

For a moment the two rejected suitors stood paralysed by surprise and dismay. Then, as if the same idea had occurred to them both at the same time, they set off hastily in the direction of the village. Robert had the advantage, of course. He leapt into his car and started off with a deafening crash of gears. Throwing dignity to the winds, Jameson ran behind. There was a look of triumph on Robert's face—but it died away as the car stopped suddenly and refused to go on any further. Jameson passed him with a meaning smile and hastened on towards the village. Robert leapt from his seat, threw open the bonnet, and examined the petrol gauge. The petrol tank was empty. Without a moment's hesitation he left the stranded car and hastened in the wake of Jameson. He caught him up and, tense, silent, striding neck to neck, they made their way to the house of Mr. Bryant. Mr. Bryant was sorry, however, but the secretaryship had now been accepted by Ronald Bell. The rivals heaved sighs of relief. They did not mind Ronald Bell's having the secretaryship, but neither could have endured the other to have had it. During the interview Jameson made frequent but unsuccessful attempts to remove his hat.

"A new one," he explained at last with an unhappy laugh, "there must be something wrong with the lining, I suppose."

Robert and Mr. Bryant came to his rescue and tugged with such good will that at last the hat came away, leaving the lining still adhering to Jameson's brow like a crown.

Victor, watching through the window, knew the pure joy of an artist who sees his work to be well done.

The two rivals came out, Jameson wearing his crown and carrying his hat in his hand.

"It must be the imitation leather lining," he was saying to Robert, "it's probably made of some sort of composition and the heat of my head's melted it. I'll soak it off and send it back to the shop. I'll insist on having my money back. I've spent an awful lot on that girl."

"So 've I," said Robert mournfully, "and she went on as if it was my fault about that tin of paint. I'd had the car in the garage having a tyre mended and I suppose this tin of paint got mixed up in it then. . . ."

"It must have done," said Jameson, and added: "Her nose was too small, you know, and I don't think she's the type of woman to make a man happy."

"I don't either," said Robert. "I wish I hadn't bought those flowers."

"I bought these shoes, too," said Jameson sadly. "I've never given as much for a pair of shoes before. And then that little wretch Victor went and put brown all over the white part—making a fool of me."

"And that little wretch William went and chalked something on the back of my car," said Robert, "making a fool of me."

Jameson had the grace to look slightly abashed at this information.

"Oh, well," he said tolerantly, "boys will be boys, I suppose."

Meantime William and Victor were walking home by the field.

"Well, it's jolly well all over now," said William. "I bet I won."

"No, I did," said Victor.

"You didn't. I did."

"You didn't. I did."

"All right," said William, "let's call it equal. I'm sick of it anyway. Let's find the others and have a game."

THE END